Truth
Or
Consequences

By

Dave Turpin

This is a work of fiction. Names, characters, places, and incidents either are the product of the author's imagination or are used fictitiously. Any resemblance to actual events, locales, organizations, or persons, living or dead, is entirely coincidental and beyond the intent of either the author or publisher.

Copyright © Dave Turpin 2010
All Rights Reserved

ACKNOWLEDGMENTS

I owe a huge bill of thanks to the following people, places and things.

1. People - Gayle, Cindy, Paul, ET, Rumi, Terry, Dianne, Mike Butler and Family, Steven, Candie, California Writer's Club, Red River Writer's Club, NaNoWriMo (National Novel Writing Month). The Beast. There are so many people, thank you, this is what we accomplished!

2. Places - The Land of Enchantment, New Mexico.

3. Things - My Laptop, you are my trusted partner in all things writing! A bad dinner at a truck stop on I-40 for the kernel of an idea for this story.

Chapter 1

Vivika Stryker sat behind the wheel of her low slung customized Lexus. She heard voices. Not like someone sitting next to her in the car talking to her more like off at a distance. The voices sounded like they were coming to her through a long pipe.

Her body felt hot in places, but she also felt a chill over her entire body. Was she sleeping? "You're just dreaming." she told herself. The voices were louder now, but still didn't sound right. Whoever was talking to her in her dream didn't know how to speak English very well. She could make out single words. Bag. Deployment. Hello. All right. Air. Wait, that was airbag, wasn't it? What a weird dream. The hot spots on her body moved and increased in intensity. The whole body chill was annoying.

"I'm cold." She told herself. "Grab the blanket and pull it up, silly." What a weird dream.

Suddenly and rudely, her right leg cramped like a bitch. "Dammit!" She tried to jump out of bed and stretch the leg cramp away like her coach had taught her. But she couldn't move out of the bed and the pain from the leg cramp tripled in pain. "Dammit dammit dammit!" she cried out.

"Hang in there young lady. This is going to hurt for a few minutes."

She heard all of the words this time, loud and clear. "Wha...?" And then the pain coursed through her entire body, shoving the chill and the hot spots to one side. She screamed. And screamed some more as the EMTs held her tight on the backboard for traction as the firemen finished cutting the top off of her pretty Lexus.

"Just keep screaming! I'm glad you're awake." An anonymous EMT spoke to her as he held her hand. His partner was still working on the compound fracture of her lower tibia. The fire and rescue crew was finished with the Jaws of Life. As the team lifted her out of her now roofless luxury car, Vivika looked up at the stars and screamed some more.

* * * * *

"Do you remember anything about the accident?" A doctor with a white lab coat over green surgical scrubs asked.

"I'm not sure what I remember. I know I left the gym at 9:20, because it takes about thirty-five minutes to get home from the gym and my favorite show comes on at ten." Vivika explained.

"What's your favorite show?"

"Umm... that one with, you know, that actor and actress." She stalled out. There was a blank where the details of her favorite TV show should be.

"That's normal after so much trauma." He made a note in her chart. "Any pain or discomfort anywhere?"

"Not really pain, but I'm sore everywhere."

"That's good. Sore we can handle, pain we don't like." He made another note, stood up, and patted her gently on the shoulder. She winced.

"What happened to me? Where am I exactly?"

"You were in a car accident four days ago. Right now you're with us here in Seattle at St. George's Hospital. As soon as I think you're stable enough, you'll be moved to the Dalles Physical Rehab facility."

"Rehab? Oh Jesus that can't be good!" Her eyes ran wild with panic.

"Don't take it that way. They're set up for long term physical rehab. We're more of a general hospital. They specialize in cases such as yours, and have really fine physical therapists there. As great of physical condition as your body is in, my guess is they'll have you up walking in a few weeks."

"Walking? You mean I can't walk?"

"With all the reconstruction we did on your..."

She blanked out and didn't hear another word. She stared at the wall in front of her, just between the TV hanging from the ceiling and the pitcher of water on the table over the foot of her bed.

The doctor sensed Vivika's departure. He

made a few more notes in her chart and left.

Her next visitor, Thor Stromberg, her coach. He sat in the olive green vinyl chair under the window and waited for her to wake up. Coach Stromberg was listed as the ICE (In Case of Emergency) phone number in her cell phone and had known Vivika since she changed her name ten years ago. The shy little girl he was introduced to back then had grown up as he grew old. Now she lay in the bed without her right leg below her knee. He could not remember an amputee gymnast in the Nationals, let alone the Olympics.

The coach had been warned that when she woke up, there might be some memory loss due to the head injury. He could only sit and watch her sleep as the nurses came to check her IV drip and note her vitals as they were displayed on the monitors. He had coached her for ten years. She was tough. Tough enough to withstand the loss of her parents when she was twelve. Tough enough to refuse an offer to go back to the former Czech Republic to live with distant relatives. She would pull through this, he was sure of it. But the Nationals were in six weeks and here was the captain of his all-star team, a three-time National winner and two time Olympic alternate. Ten seconds before the car crash, she was in the best shape of her life, 5 foot 3 inch, 102 pound ball of fire, posture, and strength. But as she lay there, it seemed to him that the hospital bed swallowed her, making her look more like an infant than an eighteen year old girl.

His mind wandered to the endorsement contracts on his desk. He would have to shred them now. A new team captain would have to be chosen. No doubt Ariel Byers would demand the position be given to her. Dammit. Why did this all have to happen to him now?

Vivika stirred in the bed, blinked, and looked right at the coach. "Who are you?"

His heart sank. "I'm Coach Stromberg, Vivika. You don't recognize me?"

She pulled the scratchy hospital blanket closer to her chin. "No."

"That's okay. They said you might have trouble remembering certain things. Like an old friend or a coach."

"You're *my* coach?"

"Yes, for about eleven years." He said.

"What did you coach me at?"

"Gymnastics." The thought of her not remembering the last eleven years brought a tear to his eye, and he was immediately uncomfortable.

"Gymnastics? You think I'd remember something like that." she said.

"I'll go for now and let you rest. Maybe you'll remember your old coach in the morning." He told himself not to cry and not to come back and see her here, in this setting. He had a team to rebuild.

"That's fine. I'm very tired." She didn't like this stranger as much as she liked the doctor.

Something flashed her scrambled consciousness: don't trust this man.

"Vivika, you sleep and get better, okay?" He approached the bed to kiss her forehead, but she recoiled from his movement. "Fine, fine." He touched the bedrail as he left.

A deep sigh of relief that he was gone escaped her.

Chapter 2

Vivika stayed in the general hospital another ten days. The doctors fought a mild infection on her shortened right leg. Finally, she was given the all clear and gently transported to the shiny new rehab facility.

The attendants were amazed at her physique. One rehab specialist, Portia Connely, recognized her, and her name on the charts.

Viv looked at Portia's name tag, "Port t ah. That's an unusual name."

Portia giggled. "No silly, it's pronounced like the car, Porsche or Porsche-ah. My parents were big fans of Shakespeare."

Viv looked at her, drawing a total blank.

"We can get into that later. Let's get you feeling better and walking." Portia said.

Vivika and Portia became fast friends. Portia was on duty ten hours a day. Vivika's room was in the middle of her duty station. The days went. The months went. Portia helped in any way she could. After Vivika was finally fitted with prosthesis, she volunteered to help her find transitional housing.

Portia and Vivika looked and looked for just the right housing. Ramps, grab bars, totally disabled accessible. They found a townhouse not far from the rehab facility, only a few miles from Portia's own apartment.

Portia fought the pain and tears side by side with Vivika throughout her tortuous rehab. It wasn't like Vivika was counting or anything, but it only took her 7 months, 22 days, and 6 hours to get the "good job, you're ready to be on your own" from the Chief of Staff of the Physical Rehab facility.

"How does it feel to be free from this place?" Portia asked Vivika.

"Until my memory comes back, this is the only home I've known. And you're the only real family I have." She started to cry as she stepped forward and hugged Portia. "Just because I've been released does not mean you get to *release* me too, ya know!" The bear hug got tighter.

"I know. I'll come by for dinner this week. You go now, and enjoy a couple of days of no appointments, no sweating, and no cussing me out." Portia moved away, wiping at her tears.

"Good." Vivika snorted her nose to keep it from running. "Thursday. My place. We can order in Dim Sum."

"Perfect." She cried after each patient she worked with was "set free." To her, they were hers.

Vivika got in her new Kia and left the parking lot, remembering that she did have one appointment that week. One she wasn't sure how to handle. The settlement conference with her attorney and the tour bus company. The tour bus company's doctors had examined her the week before and concluded her recovery was done.

Yes, she would experience phantom pains and itching on the missing part of her leg and foot, but as far as an immediate recovery, she was maxed out. Long term ailments were another matter. She would be required to have a physical exam once a year for the first five years.

The traffic accident reconstruction investigators found that the tour bus company was 100% liable for Vivika's accident. Poor maintenance of the bus was cited as the major contributing factor. The night of the accident, a tour bus passed Vivika on I-5. Both vehicles traveling at legal speeds. As the bus eased forward of Vivika's car, the right front tire of the bus blew apart. It was a retread. The outer rubber casing flew off the wheel at 65 mph and crashed into the windshield of Vivika's Lexus. She may have seen it at the last instant as it impacted her car, but thankfully, she couldn't remember that either.

Once the tire blew out, the driver lost control of the bus. It spun out of the lane it was in, skidded, and flopped over on its side. No passengers died, but all of them had various injuries, scrapes, bruises, and many broken bones. The driver suffered a major stroke in the ER, leaving his right side paralyzed, and speechless.

Vivika must have reacted to the crashing intruder and jerked the steering wheel hard to the right. The highway patrol noted in their report there were no skids marks in relation to her car, just impact marks on the shoulder of the freeway before her car became airborne and slammed into a hundred year old oak, 163 feet from the lane she was traveling in.

The National Transportation and Safety Board cited the tour bus company for using an illegal tire on the bus, and for driver fatigue (he had been driving for 13 hours). The tour bus company settled with all of the passengers and was awaiting Vivika's release to settle with her.

Vivika's hospital stay was paid for. All the surgeries, five so far, were covered. Her physical rehab: totally covered. Even her living expenses so far had been covered. The settlement conference was to discuss an actual settlement. To put a period on the previous months and start down a different road.

Her attorney advised her that they would offer an up- front cash settlement with lifetime medical, and potentially a monthly payout. He also advised her to remain stoic at the meeting, and defer any questions to him.

Other than the meeting, she was on her own until Portia came to her new house. She thought she was ready for some "alone" time.

Because of her injuries, she would no longer be able to compete, and there was no chance for high dollar endorsements. Due to her current amnesia, there was little chance to pick up a coaching job. For these facts alone, the tour bus's attorneys and insurance company wanted to settle with Vivika out of court. If the case went to a jury, they surely would be looking at a multi-million dollar judgment. They wanted to approach her with a high six-figure cash payment, backing that up with a 25 year monthly payment plan.

She was restless the night before the conference. Her phantom pains kept her tossing and turning most of the night. Since the accident, her dreams were striking in their colors, movement, and texture. That night, stereo sound effects joined the mix. Her psychologist assured her this was all very normal during her healing period. With the help of a mild pain pill, she finally slept for several hours undisturbed.

Chapter 3

Vivika remained stoic through the settlement conference. Her attorney, however, put on a show. He slammed the table with his fist, snarled, and barked at opposing counsel. She thought he would blow a vein right off of his neck. He threatened to not settle per his client's wishes and force the entire matter in front of a jury. How would they like to pay out $25 million right now? Vivika sat by as her champion whooped the other team.

The settlement: full lifetime medical, $950,000 cash payment (that day), and $15,000 per month (increasing 2% per year). She was happy. Relieved that it was done. Her attorney bitched that he could have held out for a lot more, but he acquiesced so she could put it behind her.

Vivika was happy with the outcome and, on the way home, she had a flash of memory: she had been involved with attorneys once before. It was a fuzzy memory, but they were involved with the legalities of her name change. Vivika pulled off the street into a parking lot of a strip mall. She was shaking. Name change? Why couldn't she remember the details? Changing your name is a big event, but she was blank. As she sat there shaking, all the obvious questions ran through her mind: why did she change her name? What was her *real* name? How long ago did this take place? Who was involved in the decision making process? Were her parents involved? "Oh my god, what happened to my parents? Where are they? Who are they?" She called Portia. She could help.

"Portia!" Vivika's voice strained.

"Viv. What's wrong?" Instantly concerned. "Did the conference not go well?"

"No, it went fine. But I had a flashback or something. My name might not be Vivika!" She broke down and cried.

"Whoa, slow down Viv. Tell me what this flashback was all about."

Through sniffling and tears, Vivika recalled the flashback.

"Okay, listen Viv, my shift is over at three today. I'll swing by and we can go over this thing again. Just sit there for a few minutes and calm down a little before you go home."

Vivika sat in her car. She didn't know if she was alone or not. Did she have a large family somewhere? A large support group? Or was it just the creepy coach guy and Portia?

As three o'clock rolled around, Portia stopped in the file room and pulled Vivika's file. There were a few lines regarding her background, plus some pre-crash pictures that she thought might help bring her friend into a better understanding of her past.

At 3:45, Portia was greeted by a still crying Vivika, with puffy, bloodshot eyes, extra tissues in her hand. "Oh, you poor thing." Portia reached out and hugged her teary friend.

"I don't mean to be a pain in the ass. But I'm tired of not knowing who I am!"

"It's okay. I brought your file with me so I can go over it with you to see if it helps at all."

"My file?"

"Your medical file. Now, let's sit down at the table and get started."

Portia opened the file and read through the first page. Most of the information Vivika already knew. Age. Height. Weight. The vital statistics. The next few pages were post-op patient progress charts and then the pictures. "Viv these pictures are pretty graphic. They show your injury, your leg, head, bruising, and the like." She slid the photos to Vivika.

"God! That's what I looked like the night of the accident?"

"You were banged up pretty bad. So you see, you can't really blame yourself for any loss of memory or the loss of your leg. It's not like you did anything to cause the damage. You survived because of the great physical shape you're in."

"And I'm so fit because of the gymnastics?"

"Right." She thumbed through the surgeon's notes. "Nothing of much interest in these pages."

"Nothing?" Vivika asked.

"Patient is exhibiting pain and normal post-op bruising, blah blah blah." She grinned, trying to lighten the mood.

"Okay. What's next?"

"The tour bus's insurance company ran a background check on you and for whatever reason, a copy of it is in here."

"Background check?"

"More like private investigator's report."

"Seems odd, doesn't it?" Vivika asked.

"Not odd at all. The only strange thing is that a copy of it is in this file. I've come across one of these before."

"Fine, whatever. Any good news in the report?"

"Bingo." Portia scanned the report while Vivika got up and got them each a soda out of the fridge.

"Bingo?" Vivika snapped to attention.

"We now know your real name, kiddo!" Portia's voice full of excitement.

Vivika reached over and put her hand on Portia's. "Tell me."

"Your name at birth was Vivianko Strakonovich. You were born here in Seattle. Your parents were Czech immigrants. You started training at the Stromberg gym when you were six years old. Your parents..." Her voice trailed off.

"What?? What about my parents???"

"Sweetie, they passed away when you were 12. They had gone back to their hometown in the former Czech Republic and were killed in a plane crash in Russia. I'm so sorry, Viv."

She sat stunned. No parents. "Does it say

if I have any relatives at all?"

Portia skimmed a few lines. "Yes. You have an aunt on your father's side that still lives over there. I can't pronounce the name of the town." She spun the file and pointed it out to Vivika.

She looked at the town and read it aloud without hesitation.

"You can read Czech?" Portia ask.

"I, I guess so?" Her lips moved upward into a small smile.

"How about that, Viv!" Portia gave her a high five.

"Okay, that's my real name, and what happened to my parents. But why did I change my name?"

"The investigator found and made a copy of the court petition to legally change your name. Your Coach Stromberg petitioned the court six months after your parents died. In the petition it says he was seeking the change on your behalf for professional reasons. Oh I get it, like a stage name. And he makes it sound real strong and forceful."

"Why?"

"Probably to psyche out the competition. You know, here comes *Stryker* and she hasn't lost a match in three years!" Portia giggled.

"Fine. I'm okay with that, I guess."

Portia's face lost color. Vivika noticed the rapid change to expressionless. "What's the matter Portia?"

Truth or Consequences

"Umm. This next part. I, I'm not comfortable with telling you this next part."

"Why? Am I really a guy?" Vivika reversed things and she tried to lighten the mood.

"Your coach is your legal guardian. Or was until you turned eighteen. And..."

"And?"

"There is a police report in here from about four years ago. He was investigated for possible embezzlement, and child..."

"Child what? Tell me!" Vivika stood up.

"Molestation."

"Dear god, no wonder I didn't want him near me in the hospital!"

"The embezzlement was about your inheritance. The airlines paid you $500,000 for the loss of your parents. And it looks like it was all used to pay for your housing and training." Portia closed the file.

"I don't know what to say." Vivika sat in silence. Portia stayed with her throughout the night.

*   *   *   *   *

She was looking for a phone number. The brightly colored tabloid ruffled in the breeze as she sat in her car outside the convenience store. She found the phone number on the publisher's statement, and then dialed it.

"National Tab, how may I direct your call?"

"How much would you pay for a story and some pictures of a one-legged female gymnast?"

Chapter 4

They sat on the couch, absorbing the new information about Viv. Vivika fell asleep and slumped into Portia. Portia took an afghan and covered them both. Portia fell asleep after Vivika on the couch. Portia's long muscular body was cramped into the corner of the couch. She would pay the next day for the weird position her body stayed in all night. But she was there for her friend.

Vivika felt strange. Asleep, warm, and feeling safe with a warm body next to her. A body that wanted nothing from her. No sex. No talking. She was there for her. A quiet sentinel. She didn't know how long she had been sleeping when the dreams and voices started. She was driving again, at night, on a dimly lit road that didn't look familiar. Behind her, pitch black darkness. She couldn't see it, but something was slamming into the ground just behind the bumper of the car. The impact jostled the whole car. It was like a monster with giant feet was hot on her tail, trying in vain to stomp her ass right into the roadbed. She accelerated. So did the giant. The road led into and out of a tunnel, then another tunnel. The stomping noise was muffled inside the tunnels. Someone called out to her: "*Take the very next exit!*" She argued in her dream that there wasn't an exit! Nothing in sight. Just the long, dark road. She argued with the voices and shrieked each time the monster stomped its foot. The voices were of a child, an old woman, and a gruff, old man. In her dream she asked herself, "How would you know if you recognized one of these voices?" Her inner argument ensued. "But they sound safe. They sound like they know what they're talking about." She kept driving, waiting for the crash of the giant footfall. The little girl's voice pleaded: *"Miss, take the next exit please."* She hollered at the little girl, "There is no damned exit!" Vivika thought she could feel the giant's breath, but the windows were up. She took her eyes off the road for a split second to turn on the AC. The giant roared, and she could feel it's hot breath this time for sure. The kindly old woman's voice floated in next. *"Dahling take the next exit, for your sake and ours."* Vivika beat the steering wheel in her dream. Actually, it was Portia's thigh on the receiving end of her pounding fist. Portia only watched and listened. Vivika knew, just knew, the giant was timing his steps just so, and that within a few more footfalls, he would flatten her. The grumpy old man's voice boomed, *"For god's sake kid try a different direction. Go another way. You're stuck if you stay on this road. Like they all told you, take the next exit dammit!"* Suddenly, there was a flash of white light blinding her. She shielded her eyes with both hands and instinctively slammed on the brakes. The car she was driving slid to a stop and she opened her eyes. She stopped in time to see a slate gray wall with a huge double headed directional arrow, each tip pointing in opposite directions. All of the voices chimed, *"Choose!!!"*

"Son of a bitch!" Vivika shot straight up and off of the couch, eyes wild, standing with her fists balled up, glaring at nothing more than the interior of her townhouse.

"Vivika." Portia spoke softly. "Viv. I'm still here. You've had a bad dream. Vivika. Look at me." Portia sat on the edge of the couch, anticipating fleeing from a fast punch.

"Portia? Wha...?"

"It was just a bad dream. You're fine. I'm fine."

"But it was so real. Why, why am I having these damned dreams?"

"You suffered a great deal of trauma. Physically and mentally. And stupid me, I brought that file here. You've saw and heard things in there most people shouldn't ever see or hear. Add that to the meds you've taken for pain, and there's a host of reasons for the dreams. They will go away."

"When?" Vivika relaxed her fists and began trembling.

"Soon." Portia's medical training kicked in, giving pat answers to unanswerable questions.

"Not soon enough for me!"

"Look at the time. My shift starts in an hour."

"Go. I'll be okay. You can use my shower if you want. I'll bet you didn't get much sleep with me thrashing around like…"

"I'm fine. Really. You didn't start beating me until about an hour ago. I got plenty of sleep, Viv. I'll take a rain check on the shower. I'll change at work."

They hugged and exchanged promises to call each other during the day to check on one another. Portia was gone. Vivika stood with her back to the closed front door, weeping.

* * * * *

"Hello Vivika."

She answered the front door without looking out the peephole.

"What are you doing here?" she asked Coach Stromberg.

"I haven't seen or heard from you since you were in the hospital. I'm worried about you."

"You're not welcome here. Ever." She slammed the door in his face.

He knocked again.

"Leave, or I'm calling the police."

Coach Stromberg left.

* * * * *

She tapped her left foot as she was put on hold for the second time. The receptionist at the rehab facility knew who Vivika was. She saw her as a spoiled little rich girl, and that didn't cut any slack with the receptionist. Vivika Stryker wasn't anything more than another impatient patient.

"Miss Stryker, we have an opening next Thursday at four o'clock."

"Not soon enough. I want to talk to Dr. Nelson, now. Put her on the phone."

"Miss Stryker, you know it doesn't work that way. She's with a patient. Let me book you for next Thursday." Click. The phone went dead. Bitch.

Vivika drove the speed limit to the rehab facility, but she was there in half the normal time it took to get there. She parked in a "reserved" parking space and walked into the facility, passed the receptionist without hearing the shouting, and busted into Dr. Nelson's office, slamming the door behind her.

"Well, hello, Vivika. Did we have an appointment today?"

"You know we didn't. I have a couple of real quick questions for you and I'll be out of your hair."

"Okay." Dr. Nelson closed the file she was reviewing. "Shoot."

"Am I mentally and physically well enough to travel by myself?"

"How do you mean?"

"Am I gonna start slobbering at the mouth and have some sort of fit or something?"

"Not likely. Not unless you suffer another blow to the head." She waited, curious as to where the question was really leading.

"And I'm not some kind of nut? I'm not

going on a killing spree anytime soon?"

"I don't think that's in your nature, and you're not on any medicine that would cause that kind of behavior."

"So, in your opinion, if I wanted to just get in my car and take off, I could, right?"

"I don't want to see you miss any appointments, but yes, you are fit enough to take off for a few days if you want."

"No, not a few days, more like a year or two, maybe longer."

"I can't advise you to miss your appointments. You're at a very important stage in your physical therapy and…"

"Bite my ass. I'm as strong as you are. I just wanted to make sure that I'm not going to flip out or pass out. I'm done."

"I strongly suggest you reconsider. You have more work to do."

"I'll call you the next time I'm in town." Vivika turned and left Dr. Nelson's office. She stopped at the receptionist's desk. "Page Portia for me."

The receptionist shot her a go to hell look.

"NOW DAMMIT!" Vivika backhanded a pen and business card holder off the top of the counter.

"Fine, bitch. Portia, come to the receptionist desk, one of your patients is trying to escape." She smiled at Vivika.

Portia jogged to the reception area. She could tell Vivika was fit to be tied. "Viv, what's

Truth or Consequences

wrong?"

"I'm done."

"Done?"

"Done with this place, these assholes around here, this stupid ass city, the weather, the lack of good memories... all of it."

"But where, what?" She was interrupted.

"You wanna newly remodeled handicap access townhouse for cheap? I mean cheap. I'll sell it to you for a hundred bucks."

"Viv, come on, let's sit down and talk about this."

"Nope. I'm going home to pack a few things and hitting the road."

"Where are you going? When will you be back?" Portia pleaded with her eyes.

"I don't know where, and I'm more doubtful as to when. Here's the spare key. I'll leave mine under the mat."

"But,"

"I'll have an attorney contact you with the paperwork. Thank you for everything you've done for me. I'll never forget you. I hope." She pointed to her head and winked. With that, she turned without looking back, waving over her shoulder.

Portia wept as she watched not only her patient, but her friend in need, walk away.

* * * * *

After Vivika's public goodbye, Portia

took the rest of the afternoon off. She wanted some comfort food of grand magnitude. She stopped in her favorite deli on her way home. Perusing the deli selections she decided on baked beans, mac and potato salad, and a foil bag with six pieces of fried chicken in it. As she stood at the checkout stand, her eyes darted around the magazine rack. A familiar face stared back at her. Vivika's face was spread across the front page of the National Tab.

Chapter 5

Her mind made up, Vivika drove back to her townhouse. Barely waiting for the security gate at the entrance to fully open, she sped into the parking lot. She never saw the pickup truck pull in behind her through the security gate. She parked in her numbered parking space and bolted from her car to the front door. Her purse landed on the couch along with her keys. The sticking front door, slightly ajar.

In the closet, she found her old gym bag. She tossed it on the bed, and then thought about it. No, not that bag. She picked it up, crumpled it and put it in the waste basket next to the bed, then went back to the closet to find another bag. There was a smaller bag on the upper shelf. Out of habit, she jumped up to drag the bag down. Coming down a little hard on her right leg, she cringed in pain. But desire overcame the discomfort in short order. She placed the bag on the end of her bed and started retrieving clothes from her dresser. Her bras and other clothes were as small as she was. In one handful, she had seven pair of bras and panties. Into the bag followed them with a dozen pair of ankle socks, then snatched four sweatsuits from hangers, rolled them up and stowed them in the bag. She stood studying her dresser drawers, wondering what else she could force into the bag. And debating whether she should really take off.

"*Monster monster, who's got a monster.*" It was the little girl's voice from her dream. She was skipping rope and sing songing her simple rhyme, and there was a background noise. The little girl sounded like she was skipping down a long tiled hallway in tap shoes. "*Monster monster, who's got a monster.*" Vivika placed a hand on her forehead and one on her stomach. She was dizzy. No, she was nauseous.

"*Hey kid, exit now!*" the grumpy old man from the dream bellowed, his voice so loud it was if she was standing in front of a heavy metal concert speaker.

"Leave me alone!!!" Both hands holding her head shouting into the thin air of her vacant bedroom.

"Are you still talking to your imaginary friends? I thought you would grow out of that years ago." Coach Stromberg stood leaning up against the frame of the bedroom door.

The voices, and now this. She jumped, her right leg catching the edge of the mattress, and tossed her to the not-so-soft carpet.

"What in the hell are you doing here? How did you get in here? Leave now!!!" She tried to gain her composure, stand up and talk tough, while he simply stared at her.

"Going somewhere Vivika?" He walked to the bed and poked through her bag of clothes. "Looks like you're packing light. Only going for a few days?" A slimy grin crossed his lips.

"I want you to leave now!" She began

edging toward the phone on the nightstand.

"Obviously you invited me in. Otherwise, the door would be closed."

"Monster monster Viv's got a monster."

"I'm calling the police."

"Oh, those guys again. Go ahead. You must have forgotten the last couple times. Go ahead and call. I'll wait." He sat down on the bed and plucked a pair of panties out of her bag. "Nice." He held them to his face.

"Dahling, sweet dahling, exit now."

She made it to the phone. "Do you need the phone number?" He stood up.

"I've seen the file. I know you molested me."

"They investigated me, and you, and found nothing. No charges."

"So you admit it?"

"Nothing ever happened between us. But you wouldn't remember right now." He moved closer.

"Stay back." She dialed 911.

He stopped in his tracks. "I thought we could work things out. We always have in the past."

A faint voice from the earpiece on the phone, "911 what's your emergency? Hello?"

"Spooky, now *I'm* hearing voices. Okay Vivika, I guess I'll go for now." The six foot hulk of a man in his zippy sounding track suit turned to leave. "Oh, don't forget our anniversary is in about a week. I thought we could go out for a nice dinner on the lake cruise."

"Anniversary?" The nausea made her fold her body forward.

"You forgot that too? My dear little bride, our first wedding anniversary is on the sixth. Tisk tisk tisk, I thought for sure you'd remember that." He walked out of the bedroom.

The 911 operator was busy notifying the nearest patrol unit that she had an unresponsive call.

Vivika's body couldn't stand up another second. She collapsed onto the bed and slipped to the floor.

"*Monster monster who's got a monster...*" Vivika passed out.

* * * * *

"Hey kid time to wake up." The grumpy old man whispered to her, startling her awake. "Fine I'm awake leave me alone!" She pried herself up on the edge of the bed and noticed her bag, half packed, half unpacked. Vivika moved slowly to add a few more items to the bag and redeposit the items that the asshole removed. She took another look around the room. If she needed anything, she'd buy it. The handles of the bag hooked under her arm comfortably as she snatched it and headed for her tidy kitchen. She opened the fridge, grabbed a large bottle of water, and left the townhouse. She closed and locked the door, and walked to her car. As Vivika drove out

of the security gate, a marked patrol car came in through it. The cop car never even registered. Part of her already gone, and now the rest of her could catch up.

An hour later, heading south on Interstate 5, she would have to explain to the nice officer that she was fine. A BOLO (Be On the Look Out) had been issued after the responding officer could not locate her at her residence. Thirty minutes of assuring the officer she was fine and that the 911 call was just a mistake and that it would never happen again, and no she had not been drinking or doing drugs and no there was no intruder, he reluctantly released her. He sent her on her way. In his report, he noted that the subject seemed calm, coherent, and not under the influence.

On her run to her new life, she saw herself as a car-bound Forrest Gump. He ran and ran. She was alone in her KIA, a single CD and the radio to keep her company. She stopped once in Northern Oregon to gas up and grab a few road snacks: Corn Nuts, a Slim Jim, peanut M&M's, a Slurpee and she was back on the road. Her vision of where to end up was a little hazy to say the least. Just as hazy was the statement about her wedding anniversary. A girl should remember her wedding day, right?

Having apparently grown up in a big city, Vivika thought maybe it was time for a smaller venue. Smaller town, smaller pressures. She went over and over in her mind what the voices kept saying about "exit now". Wasn't watching Seattle fade out of sight in her rear view mirror an exit? Going a different direction?

*   *   *   *   *

"Portia, I cannot stress how disappointed I am in you. You know how important patient confidentiality is. This is the second time this year patient photos and stories have been leaked to the press." Dr. Nelson, her angry face flushed red, raged at Portia. "I demand an explanation. Not to mention how fired you are."

"I have no explanation. I can only say I had nothing to do with that." Portia pointed to the National Tab that lay face up on Dr. Nelson's desk in front of her.

"You were the last person to check into the records room. You were the last person seen on video surveillance. And you sit there and tell me you had nothing to do with it?"

"I admit that I did take Vivika's file out, and yes, I did take it to her the other night. She was having a major problem and I thought the file would answer some of her questions. The security video and logs should show that I returned it to the records room the next morning."

"Yes, the records and tape confirm that. And you still deny releasing the photos in her file to these jerks?"

"Absolutely I deny it."

"Can you explain how the file pictures ended up on as headlines?"

"Seems far-fetched, but someone must have taken the file from my car, made copies, and sent the results to the tabloid. It's the only thing I can think of."

"I think we're done here. Security is waiting outside. Clean out your locker and leave the premises. Our attorney will be in touch soon." Dr. Nelson dismissed Portia with a limp wave of her hand.

Portia stepped to the door, "You said this was the second time this year that this has happened?"

"Yes."

"When?"

"January."

"I started working here in mid-February." She opened the door and slammed it closed behind her.

*   *   *   *   *

Three months after her swift departure, Vivika called her attorney and instructed him to transfer title and ownership of her condo to Portia immediately. Overnight the paperwork and she'd make sure it was notarized. Vivika reminded him to make sure he filled out Form 1179, part c and d, so Portia would have a soft landing with her tax liabilities. She held the phone away from her ear.

"How did I know to tell him all of that?"

Her business acumen came from years of

being the coach's office manager. While he siphoned funds from her trust fund to shore up his gym, she learned how to run the business. Another reason for the marriage, the old "A wife cannot be forced to testify against her husband clause."

Chapter 6

Several years, thousands of miles, and a change of vehicles, Vivika was done. She had driven up and down the eastern seaboard, spent nights along the Gulf Coast, made a large loop up to the Canadian border, and fallen in love with New Mexico's Land of Enchantment. Just like Forrest on his long run, she came to a stop on the southbound shoulder of Interstate 25. She guessed she was somewhere between Socorro and Las Cruces, New Mexico. She normally reviewed the atlas only in the mornings, to get a general overview of where she thought she might be heading that day.

She didn't know why she stopped. All she knew for sure was, she, like Forrest was done. Done? Yes, done. She sat in the fairly new 4Runner she had purchased after a grueling snowstorm in North Dakota. Come to find out, her wonderful little KIA didn't like snowstorms much. With the new SUV though, she spent the extra bucks and made sure it had satellite radio, a 10 CD changer and a docking station for her new laptop.

The first couple of months, she traveled like she felt inside, a blank page. No plan, no map. Just drive. She stopped to sleep or eat. Then the idea came to her that she should keep a daily journal. In case she ever lost her memory again, at least she would have a springboard into recovery.

Into the journal she added notes about favorite places she drove through or stayed. And an entire section on her *new* favorite foods and more or less how to prepare them. The rest was just a basic journal: I hate this. I hate that. I wonder what I did then? What about that marriage thing? I wonder how long these voices have been haunting me? Will they ever go away?

"Don't be silly dahling..."

They were still with her and showed up at the best and worst times.

There was a knock on the driver's side window. "Miss, are you all right" The officer gave the window another knuckle rap. "Miss!"

She was lost in thought, staring at a huge outcropping of ancient rocks off in the distance.

"Miss! Hello!!" His voice got louder.

Vivika slowly turned and looked at him, like *he* was the freak on the side of the road. "What?"

"Roll the window down please."

"What? Is there something wrong?" She asked.

"I'm supposed to ask you that." He smiled and took a quick glance around the inside of her SUV. Junk food wrappers, empty Slurpee cups, a laptop, and other traveling necessities. He took note of her age and overall condition. "Is everything all right in there?"

"Yes, of course it is." She looked around.

Messy, but otherwise fine. "Why do you ask?"

"You've been sitting here about an hour. I passed you on my patrol going north, and you're still here an hour later. Part of the job, ya know."

"I was distracted and thought I would stop for a few minutes. I guess the time just got away from me. I'll just go."

"Now, I have to do the other part of my job and ask for your license, registration, and ask you if you've been drinking today?"

She giggled and flashed a broad smile. "I haven't been drinking today at all." She dug into her purse and produced her license, reached into the glove compartment and handed him the registration.

"Ok, sit tight. I'll be right back."

She fidgeted. Changed the channels on the radio. Reached and took a long draw on the straw in her latest Slurpee mixture of blueberry and strawberry. Her lips and tongue showed the results.

Officer Montez returned to her window. "Everything seems to be fine. When was the last time you slept?"

"Strange question, isn't it?"

"I have to ask. Looking at your current nutritional choices, sleep is probably not high on your list either."

"I slept yesterday, like normal people."

He caught a slight hesitation in her voice. "Yesterday. Where?"

"Umm, let's see." She was stumped. It was either Kansas or Colorado. "North of here."

"Tell you what. I'm going to pull ahead of you and I want you to follow me to the exit up ahead. It's only a few miles. I think you should stop for the day and get some rest."

"I guess that would be ok." What an odd cop she thought.

"Dahling, just follow the handsome young man."

"Oh just shut up!"

He was a half a stride away when he heard her. "Pardon me?"

"Oh nothing. I was arguing with the... radio report."

"Fine, fine, just follow me."

Vivika waved him on, and then followed him to the next exit. A large weathered billboard shouted greetings. "WELCOME TO TRUTH OR CONSEQUENCES NEW MEXICO!!!"

"Ha, that's fitting." Grumpy chimed in.

She followed the officer as he pulled into the first motel parking lot in town. "I guess he was serious."

He parked his patrol car, came over to her vehicle, and escorted her to check-in.

"Hey Billy, how the heck are you?" The motel clerk behind the counter greeted Officer Montez.

"Hey Barb, just fine. Say, I stopped to see if you have a room available for a weary traveler?"

"You bet. I'll even give you the corporate rate."

"It's not for me. It's for Miss, I'm sorry is it Miss or Mrs. Stryker?"

"Miss." Vivika perused the brochure stand. Pamphlets and brochures screamed all sorts of come-ons. From the large radio array, to a civil war battle site and a walking tour of cliff dwellings. Another, shouted, "Look at me! Look at me!" for Elephant Butte Lake.

"One night?" Barb asked.

"That should be fine." Officer Montez replied.

"Do you have a room if I decided to stay for a week?"

"You bet Miss Stryker. Shall I put you down for a week?" The off season was a bitch, so Barb wrote up the slip fast.

"Fine, make it a month then." Vivika waved the go-ahead, again.

"Find something you like?" Officer Montez stepped over to where Vivika was studying the brochures.

"Lot's of potential. Have you ever been to this array thing?"

"A bunch of times. It used to be on my patrol." He smiled.

"How about these hot springs?" She read the headline on one pamphlet that swore to the magical healing powers of the hot mineral spring baths.

"You have to experiment. Each one has a

different tub, different ways to control the water temperatures. I suggest going to several. Since you'll be here a while, you could try one per day. People come from around the country to take a dip in the hot springs."

"Interesting."

Barb handed back her charge card along with the room key. "Thanks for staying with us. If there is anything you need, just call the desk. Stop in anytime, Billy."

"Thanks Barb."

Montez walked Vivika back out to her SUV. "Well, you're in good hands. Here's my card in case you have any questions about the local area or travel questions." He grinned.

She looked at the state issued business card. Officer B.J. Montez. "Ok, I guess I better go to my room and go to bed like a good little girl."

He gave an ok sign and walked to his patrol car. As he opened the car door, "One last question…"

"Yes?" She swung open the hatch to the rear of her SUV.

"Have we ever met before?"

She hesitated, waiting for the voices to spout off something smartass. "I don't think so. Never been here before today."

"K, I, S, S, I, N, G… skip skip skip to my…"

"No problem. Take care." He was in the cruiser and gone.

Chapter 7

Vivika unloaded her SUV into the motel room. She was going to stretch out on the bed for a little while, and then go have a late lunch, but, she woke up at noon the next day when housekeeping knocked on her door. Almost 24 hours of pure sleep. No dreams and her boisterous friends held their tongues all night for a change. As she was taking her shower Vivika surmised they were all tired. When she was dressed, she took inventory of her clothes bag. She *really* needed to do laundry. Between the B.O. and the Slurpee stains, she was way overdue on having clean clothes. Vivika sat on the edge of her bed and felt like she was wide awake for the first time since she left Seattle all those months ago. Her nails needed tending to, a mani and pedi for sure was on the "to do" list for the day. Her comfy warm up suits were dated and worn. Her tennis shoes were scuffed and needed replacing. She made it to the mirror over the sink. The weird light from the buzzing overhead fluorescents couldn't hide her hair. "Oh my god. Enough of this shit!" On the way out the door she grabbed the laundry. It was time to come back to her body.

Vivika's favorite food was fresh stir fry, but she soon found the main selections of dining in central New Mexico, strangely enough, leaned toward Mexican food. Home style, old fashioned,

Americanized, fresh Mex, Tex-Mex, and to top it off, she had to constantly decide between red or green chili sauce.

After her lunch, where she opted for a chicken fajita skillet, which was out of this world good, she sought out a hair salon. Vivika discovered rather painfully that her choices were slim for a fresh styling. Cuts by the Creek, Bo's Cut and Blow, and Johnny's Barber Shop. Generally no walk-ins, and all were only open three days a week.

Johnny's Barber Shop got her business. She decided in the end that it was not an unpleasant experience. Surrounded by big burly men, Vivika heard details about an upcoming Elk hunt, the latest goings-on out at the Turner Ranch, and Mel's prostate surgery, which had the heft of importance and reverence. Johnny's damn grandkid was busted again; the fishing report from Elephant Butte Lake was dismal. A curious significant point of interest seemed to be most of the men were Veterans of WWII, Korea, or Vietnam. They wore black caps, adorned with gold embossed embroidery announcing in which war they served, and when. She realized she felt safer than she ever had before, just being with them. These burly men would not let anything happen to her.

Johnny the barber cleaned her hairstyle with a scissor cut.

"Visiting the area?" His voice had a kind, grandfatherly tone.

"Yes. I'll be here about a month." The leather barber chair, probably 100 years old, nearly swallowed her.

"Oh that's great. You'll love it here. Lots of places to see. Not much in the way of a *scene* for young people like yourself though. Mostly just old retired farts."

A man waiting his turned barked, "Watch it Johnny. I might be retired, but I ain't no damned old fart!"

"Marv, you're 92 years old. You passed old fart 30 years ago!" Johnny shot back. The patrons all laughed in unison. His eyesight limited, Marv went back to looking at the pictures in the six month old hunting magazine he was holding.

"He's a sweetheart." Johnny commented to Vivika as he returned his focus to her bangs with the scissors. "Don't miss going to the hot springs. We have a bunch to choose from."

"I've heard that. Any suggestions?"

"You kind of have to experiment. My wife and I like two or three real well and we rotate going to them."

"Ok, I'll check a few of them out. Thanks for the info."

He held a few strands of her hair in his hand and looked at her in the mirror. "You haven't been eating right, have you?" Still holding her hair, his aged eyes stared into hers. "And you're not sleeping enough are you?"

"Wha... how can you tell?"

"Your hair told on you. Poor diet will show up with brittle hair and lack of sheen. It just feels unhealthy. And look at your eyes, like a road map of unhappiness."

"But..."

"No buts little miss. I've been cutting hair since I got out of the Navy back in 1958. Seen a lot of hair and lots of faces. Barbers are a lot like bartenders. But mostly my customers are sober." He smiled in the mirror at her.

"I plan on making some changes. I've been traveling a lot."

"Changes for the good I hope?" He finished her haircut and leaned down to whisper in her ear, his eyes still locked on hers. "No charge for this trim, and promise you'll stop back in here in about three weeks." He winked at her.

She smiled and nodded.

With a flourish, Johnny removed the nylon drape from her, and flung her cut hair to the floor. She stood and moved for a closer look in the mirror. He was right. Her hair looked like shit and the lines on her face looked like the atlas in her SUV. She turned to him and gave him a hug and a childlike smooch on the cheek. "I'll see you soon, Johnny."

"Okay, which one of you old farts is next? Marv, can you walk this far?"

"Johnny, respect your elders or I'll whoop yer gall dern ass!" It took Marv three minutes to get into the barber chair.

The high tone tinkle bell sounded as

Vivika opened the door.

"Funny funny old people smell funny... skip skip skip."

Vivika didn't bother telling the little girl to shut up.

*   *   *   *   *

"Red or green?" The young Latina waitress asked Vivika.

"Which one do you like?"

"Depends on what I'm eating. You ordered the house special, hmm I'd go with red sauce on that."

"That's what I'll have." Vivika smiled, and it was easier. Maybe it was the new "do".

"Cool. I'll have that right up."

On her second day, she found herself feeling more at home. She couldn't remember if she *ever* felt at home before. But doubted it. This feeling would come through even if she was in a coma.

Vivika sat staring out the window next to her table, elbows planted on the table, chin resting on the backs of her hands. Other than some haze on the horizon, she could see for miles. Compared to the verdant greens of the Pacific Northwest, the desert was awash with different colors and textures. Soft rolling foothills of sand and up- shooting, sharp cliffs, and mesas. She drifted away in the beauty.

"Here you go, the house special with red

sauce. And I brought you a small dish of green sauce so you could try it with your supper."

"Wow, thanks a bunch."

"You're welcome. Anything else?"

"I'm good, this is fine."

"Just between us girls, Johnny did real good on your hair." She smiled and walked back to wait on another customer.

Vivika ate in blissful inner silence. Halfway through her scrumptious meal of carne steak asada, some sort of internal calendar reminder went off. It was time to call her attorney for her quarterly mail forwarding request. Some time in her first sixth months on the road, she contacted the attorney with instructions to open all formal business mail, pay bills, and handle any other matters of that nature, but stack and store any personal looking mail. Every three months or so she'd call in and have him overnight what built up over the previous months. It was that time again.

In the last seven bundles of mail, Portia mailed letter after letter. Vivika left them unopened. Coach Stromberg also mailed her a couple of letters, those too left unopened in the bottom of the mailing box.

Lunch was over. Time to move around, and explore Truth or Consequences.

Chapter 8

Vivika's first complete tour of T or C lasted all of fourteen minutes. One main street through the town. At the north end, a new and shiny Wal Mart. Downtown was definitely old town. The south end was the south end of a north bound town. A few old houses and several gas stations. She was done with the main part of the tour. Lots of side streets to drive up and down. A golf course. The raging trickle of the Rio Grande River. That covered it.

It was still daylight, so she thought today was the day to start the hot springs sampling. Johnny the barber said the hot spring establishments were everywhere, 10 or 15 of them. Just drive around town or pick up one of the tourist maps and go for it.

She turned off the main street, went down a block, made another turn, and a blaring bright green hand painted sign indicated she had just found Bill & Edith's Hacienda Hot Springs. To her it looked like the hotel in Psycho. Wrought iron fencing encircled the sandy compound. A bag of bones covered in deep dark wrinkled skin sat in a lawn chair on the porch. She honestly couldn't tell if it was Bill or Edith. Whichever one it was waved a hearty greeting from their perch.

"Stay out of the deep end kid!" The Grumpy voice advised.

"Yeah yeah whatever. Maybe I'll drown all of you." What the hell. New direction right?

"Howdy hon!" It was Edith after all.

"Hi. I've heard a lot about these hot springs. Thought I'd give one a try." Vivika said, trying hard to keep the creeped out, out of her voice.

"Well sure hon. You bring a towel?"

"Nope. Left the hotel without one."

"Not a problem. Only fifty cents to rent'cha one. And it's seven-fifty for a half hour."

"Sounds fine." She was only guessing.

"C'mon, I'll sign you in and show you around."

Vivika followed Edith into the front office. She stood waiting for Edith to round the counter, amazed by the collection of oddities lining the walls and hanging from the ceiling. Stuffed and mounted birds, feathers, kites, old bottles, wind chimes, candles, and old license plates. There were stacks on the floor with the same type of mish mashed collectables.

"Read this over hon and sign at the bottom." She handed Vivika a pen.

"What is this?"

"A release, stating you don't have any glass containers, you'll not be drinking in the hot springs, basic stuff." Edith smiled.

Vivika skimmed through the release. "No drugs. No alcohol. No more than two people per room. Clothing optional." She stopped reading. "Clothing optional?" she asked.

"Sure. Some people look at it like taking a bath. Some folks prefer a swimsuit. Not a problem either way. Bill always goes in and sprays the tubs down with bleach anyways. Some folks can get pretty, umm, frisky in there."

Great endorsement. I would have kept that one to myself. New direction, right? She signed the release.

"You want a candle or two for in there?"

"Is it that dark?"

Edith let out a belly laugh. "No hon. Some people like to set a mood. I make them myself, out back, out of beeswax. I only have two scents left, bay leaf and licorice."

Viv thought she left one off the list, body odor.

"Maybe next time." Viv said politely.

"Suit yourself. Okay hon, follow me. Here's your towel."

She followed Edith back outside and down the porch to room number four. Swampy heat hit her in the face as Edith opened the door. The dimly lit room was sizable. A large concrete tub was built into the floor. The southwestern paint scheme she was growing used to splashed around the room, salmon pink, turquoise, and for good measure, a gaudy almost fluorescent green stripe went around the walls of the room. She could almost see Bill painting the walls.

Edith stepped to the tub in the floor, and then stepped down into the concrete pit. "I'll start filling it and show you how to empty it when you're done with your soak." Edith reached for a huge red valve and turned it with little effort. Water gushed out of a three or four inch pipe protruding from the wall. "This is your drain stopper." Edith held a three foot length of white plastic pipe, big around as Vivika's right leg. "You put this over the drain in the floor like this. Let the water fill up and when you're done pull up the pipe and the water drains out. If you want the water cooler, reach up here and turn this handle and cold water comes out, see." Edith turned another valve above her head and water shot down into the tub. "That's it hon. Enjoy yourself. You look like you could use a good soak." Edith left the room, pulling the door closed behind her.

The hot mineral water kept gushing as Vivika decided on whether or not she *really* needed a soak. "What the hell?" She stripped down to skin, moved closer to the edge of the tub, took her titanium prosthesis off, and tried to ease into the naturally heated mineral water.

"OH MY GOD!" She hollered as she tried to get away from the 102 degree water. "How the hell do people soak in this shit?" There was about a foot of hot water in the tub. She hopped and balanced herself as she reached for the cold water valve, turned it on, then slipped back to the steps of the tub and waited as the waters mingled. A toe test proved the water temperature safe, so she moved into the depths of the tub. She mellowed, as did the water temperature. The water level came up and overflowed into the generic drain tube. She turned the water off and soaked, and soaked. Vivika enjoyed the hot mineral spring water. For the next twenty minutes, she languished and floated until every fiber of her retired athletic body seemed to separate from each other. Each joint spread away from the other. The phantom pains in her right leg disappeared. Was she in heaven? It didn't matter. This might be better, she thought. Silence of the body, and mind, the spirit calm, and the damn voices, shhhh.

"Hon." Edith knocked on the door. "You only have five minutes left. That's a good long soak for your first time in the hot water. I wouldn't stay in there much longer."

Vivika's self-imposed world deprivation was no more. "Fine. I'll be right out."

"You might be dizzy when you get out of the tub. Watch your step. I have some ice water waiting for you."

"Thank you." She righted herself from her float position, pushed the drain tube off of the drain in the floor, and the water rushed downward. True to Edith's warning, she was lightheaded for sure. She struggled to towel off, get dressed, and walk outside. The stark contrast from the swampy heat into the cool dry desert afternoon was titillating. There was an extra lawn chair next to Edith's with a tall glass of ice water on a table between the two. "Wow. What an experience!" Vivika slumped into the lawn chair and reached for the ice water.

"Yeah, I hear that a lot. Folks do get addicted to the *soak*."

"That would be an easy thing to do. Wow." Limp as a dish rag, she sat still, holding the cold glass to her forehead. "Wow."

Edith giggled and continued cutting wicks for her next batch of candles.

Vivika sat with Edith and sipped her ice water for another half an hour. Edith filled her in on the desert rat lifestyle. "We have two speeds here, slow and slower. The desert, like the hot springs, gets under folks' skin. Almost all of them want to stay, but only a few do. That's what happened to me and Bill. Came to visit his brother staying at the VA. His brother passed away and we stayed. Next month we'll have been here, twenty-six years." She smiled at some personal memory.

"Edith, it's been a great pleasure meeting you. Thank you for the ice water and that, that hot mineral water stuff. I'll see you soon."

"Hope so. Nice to meet you hon. Take better care of yourself, ok?" Edith waved.

Vivika waved back.

"Dahling... next time you need to get a man in hot water."

"You know what, I think you're right." She grinned to herself as she pulled out of the parking lot.

Chapter 9

Vivika turned out onto the main street, still stoned from the effects of the hot spring, and all hell broke loose. A super bright light lit up the interior of the SUV, blinding her. Then a siren. Then flashing red lights.

"What the fu...?" Her voice trailed off as she quickly pulled to the curb and parked.

Officer Montez walked up to the driver's side window, which was already down. "Good evening Miss Stryker."

"Oh it's you! You scared the shit out of me you ass!"

"I wanted to see how awake you were." He grinned.

"Well you spoiled my trip to the hot springs!" She didn't want to, but she cracked a sly smile.

"You get some sleep?" He glanced around the interior.

"Yes thank you. I slept until noon today."

"And got a new haircut I see."

"How can you tell? My hair is still wet!"

"Small town."

"Oh, one of your old hunting buddies?"

"Something like that. So did you like the hot springs?"

"It was almost orgas-" She corrected herself. "It was great."

"You really needed it. You were wound

up pretty tight."

"Good way to put it. So, you're just out harassing tourists tonight or what?"

"On patrol, just doing my job." He turned and motioned with his arm. "You can see all the traffic out here that I have to keep under control." A lonely beat up Ford truck squeaked and rumbled by.

"Tough job. Well I need to go get some more rest before I get arrested for loitering."

"Tomorrow is my day off. Wanna get some lunch?" He asked staring at the ground, avoiding eye contact.

"What, and lose out on my beauty sleep? No way." She put the SUV in drive and started moving ahead.

He stood there, mouth torqued in surprise.

She stopped and poked her head out the window. "Give me a call around eleven in the morning and I'll see if I'm up to it." She pressed hard on the accelerator, and the tires let out a loud bark.

He turned, smiling to himself and made his way back to his cruiser.

When Vivika got back to the hotel, Barb came out of the office with a large white FedEx box. "This came for you today."

"Thanks Barb. It's just some forwarded mail."

"Wow." Her face showing curiosity.

"Junk mail from home." She smiled; in fact she was still smiling when she got out of her

SUV.

For the first time in recent memory she was stepping lighter, even with 30 pounds of mail. Barb's curiosity didn't even faze her. She headed for her room with plans to catch up on her mail.

Her attorney was adept at sorting her mail. He circle filed the junk and obvious crap. The "You may already be a winner." crud. The rule of thumb was, if she didn't enter a contest, how could she win, and he knew that she never bothered entering anything. The mail he did forward to her was separated, bundled, and had a note identifying what each bundle held: personal, business, and miscellaneous.

Vivika's mood was light. She was relaxed and ready to plow through the piles of mail. She laid everything out, grabbed another bottle of water out of the micro-sized fridge, came back to the bed, and flopped cross-legged, to dig into the project. The business mail was first. Financial statement. Good. Quarterly taxes paid, along with admin fees for the attorney and accountants. A letter from her financial manager suggesting a better retirement account and advising it might be time to do a touch-less transferring because the projected rates were stronger. Fine. The annual car insurance was due. A printout of all payments made on her behalf. Good good. No serious-looking problems to deal with, a signature here and there, approve or disapproval of this plan. She zipped through the business bundle in a blistering 45 minutes. For her, that was an improvement of four days and seven hours.

She hesitated with the personal bundle of mail. Picked it up. Set it back down. She opted to go through the miscellaneous mail next. Junk junk and more junk. One or two catalogs that should not have been forwarded did catch her eye. After thumbing through them and circling several items, she put those on the night stand for later. Donation requests came in from an inner city all girl gymnastics team, animal rights, environmental rights, save the sharks, a couple of Christian boys and girls homes, and a real estate magazine. The last one was a stumper. Why would the attorney include that thing?

Another personal record shattered. The miscellaneous bundle done, in 30 minutes. Her butt and bladder needed a quick break before tackling the ugly bundle, the personal mail.

"Skip skip, skip to my Lou."

"Good idea, let's go for a walk."

Viv finished her business, stretched, and headed outside into the night for a walk. She hadn't noticed in the daylight that at this end of town, there weren't what you would call sidewalks lining the streets. Dirt trails alongside the curb was about it. She bent over and touched her toes, then stretched back into a far reaching arch. Her body smiled. That felt good. She walked out to the edge of the parking lot. To her right, the road raised uphill for half a mile. To her left, the road eased downhill a quarter mile then disappeared around a curve. Vivika decided to go uphill, then make a u-turn, head to the bottom of the hill, and have a cup of hot cocoa at the Hilltop Grill. Up she went. Although it was officially nighttime, there were enough lights from a scattering of street lights and parking lot lighting that the dirt trail was easy to follow. At the top of the hill, it dawned on her, an unabated supply of Slurpees and no physical therapy was a bad combination. The dry desert air was wreaking havoc on her lips, leaving them chapped and peeling. She would attend to that in the morning. She wondered what the elevation was. The cool night air was sharp going in out of her trachea. Her lungs were slightly on fire and she was breathing hard when she topped out near the north / south Interstate 25.

"Whew." Vivika stood still for a few minutes catching up to herself. Once she regained some semblance of composure, she headed back downhill toward her reward, that cup of hot cocoa. And it was delicious. She and her imaginary friends headed back to the hotel room.

Back in the hotel room, she removed her hoodie and flopped again on the bed. The personal bundle was all that was left to go through. It was a short stack. Ten letters, all from Portia. In the past, she had ignored the letters. Left them unopened in a box in the SUV. But tonight, this night, it was time to suck it up and read all the letters. She went out to the SUV and retrieved the four small bundles of letters, brought them back to the bed, and date sorted them, so she could read them from the beginning to the current batch.

Dear Viv,
I'm not sure where you are, or what you're doing, but I hope you are well. I think about you every other minute. I want to call you, but your pit bull attorney said it was out of the question. He wouldn't even tell me which state you were in! I don't know how to say thank you for the condo, but if you ever change your mind and want it back I will understand. I have a new job. A better one in fact. I'm training for a tri-athalon. I come home after working out and die on the bed. I never thought I'd need grab bars in the shower until I was in my 80s, but lately they've come in handy. How about an email addy? I won't intrude and ask for a cell number.
Love and Hugs to you my friend,
Portia

Vivika fell fast asleep after the ninth letter.
"*Nighty night don't let the bed bugs bite.*"

*   *   *   *   *

"*Hey kid is that the boogie man?*"
Vivika shot up from her deep sleep. She looked at the alarm clock, 9:30 am. Another ten hours of sleep. Her mind, shrouded in a sleepy

Truth or Consequences

fog, she looked down at her hand. "I must have fallen asleep with Portia's next letter in my hand." She turned her hand and looked at the unopened envelope. The name on the return address label: Stromberg. She threw the envelope across the room.

The knock at the door sent her off the bed and in a full fighting stance. "Who is it??" She shouted.

"Housekeeping." A woman's voice. It was a good start.

Vivika stepped lightly to the peephole. It was housekeeping. "Can you come back around noon?"

"Sure can. Thanks."

She whispered under her breath, "No, thank you."

Before she could decide what to do next, the phone rang. The hair stood up on the back of her neck. She backed up into the wall and stared at the phone. It seemed to ring forever. When it finally fell silent, the red light on the face of the phone started to blink, letting her know she missed a call.

Chapter 10

"What news do you have for me?" Six foot tall Coach Stromberg sat down in a chair across the desk from a man in a black turtleneck sweater.

"Like I told you when you first called me, I didn't want to take this case. It doesn't pass my smell test." He tossed an envelope across the broad desk. "Here's your retainer back."

"What's your problem? My wife is missing and you're refusing to help find her?" He snatched up the envelope and put it in his jacket pocket.

"Look Mr. Stromberg, I did some preliminary investigating and your wife is not a missing person."

"Oh really? Then where the hell is she?" He scooted to the edge of his chair.

"The police made contact with her the day she left Seattle. There has been some activity with her bank accounts and a source tells me she's alive and well."

"Where is she? I have a right to know."

"Please sit back down." The man in the black turtleneck shifted his weight in his chair. "Sit, back down." A calm firm tone in his voice. "Legally, she has the right not to be found, by you or anyone else for that matter. She has her right to privacy. I really suggest you sit back down Mr. Stromberg." He leaned forward away from the back of his chair.

"Listen up, I want to find her and I want to find her now. I can pay you whatever you want. I love her and miss her. I don't understand why you won't do this for me. Or at least for the cash?" Stromberg bellowed and took a step around the desk.

"You need to sit down or leave my office." The private investigator's placid coolness was resolute.

"Do you know who I am?" Stromberg shouted.

He giggled before he answered. "I get that a lot. I don't give a flying fuck who you think you are. You have ten seconds to leave this office, and I suggest you never come back!" A rift in the coolness.

"Or what? You lay a hand on me and I'll own you."

Another hushed chuckle. "If I had a nickel for every time... Listen asshole, just leave, and forget about your wife. If I did know where she was, you'd never hear it from me. My source clued me on you and, from what I've heard, you're a worthless piece of human flesh. So just leave."

"Umhp. I'm gonna kick your-"

Before he could finish his verbal and physical threat, the man in black stood up, his right hand grabbing Stromberg's nose between his index and middle finger. He clamped down and twisted breaking the coach's nose, and rendering Stromberg blind and helpless in a nano second. "Let me show you to the door." He gathered up the material on Stromberg's jacket and ran him head first into the door frame. "Ooops. Forgot to open the door." He drew the coach back as he opened the door for him. The man in the black turtleneck flung the coach through the doorway. As his body passed by, he kicked him hard in the ass, sending the bleeding, blinded six foot man skittering on the hard porcelain tile floor in his outer office.

"Mandy, let me know if he doesn't leave right away." He winked and grinned and went back to his desk.

His receptionist stood up and peered down over her desk at the coach. She sat back down, shook her head, then took a black marker out of her desk organizer and added a mark to her bulletin board, adding the mark next to the other eight that were already there.

* * * * *

Portia folded her latest letter, slipped it into another birthday card for Vivika, and mailed it on the way to work. She worried constantly about her former patient and friend.

* * * * *

Vivika stood frozen, fixated on the phone. It began to ring again.

Truth or Consequences

"Dahling answer the damnable thing."

Robotically she moved to the phone. "Hello?"

"Vivika, it's Officer Montez. Sorry I'm calling earlier than you said, but it's such a nice day, god I hope I didn't wake you?" There was true nervousness in his voice.

"Hmm no, I'm up, and yes you did call almost two hours early!" She was rattled, but it wasn't his fault.

"I'm so sorry. We can put this off 'til another day if you want?"

"I'm ok. Can you call me back in about forty-five minutes?"

"Absolutely. I'm sorry if I disturbed you."

"I'm disturbed, but it's not your fault. Talk to you in a little bit."

"Sure thing. Bye." He had no idea what the problem was, but it immediately bothered him.

Vivika sat on the edge of the bed for a few minutes before taking a deep breath. She shook off the webs from the boogie man threat, and jumped up and into action. A hot shower, followed by a fresh change of clothes, and then she could wait for another phone call.

She didn't wait long. With a towel still wrapped around her hair, she heard the phone ring. She bounded over and answered it without hesitation.

"Hello?"

"It's me again. Officer Montez."

"And I thought it was another survey."

"Well sort of. What would you like to eat?"

"I've had nothing but Mexican food so far." She said, and then realized that might be his favorite food. Dammit.

"I hear ya. Not much of a selection in this little town."

"I didn't mean-"

"Not a problem. Hey, have you ever had an Indian Taco?"

"Never even heard of such a thing." Something moved in her memory. "Are they made with real Indians?" She laughed.

"With or by?" He returned her laugh.

"Indian tacos sound fine. Come pick me up." She was talking with her hands and scrunching her shoulders as she spoke to him.

"Be there in ten. Bye."

"God kid what have you done?"

"I know huh."

By the time Vivika arrived back at her room later in the day, she would find out a little bit of what she'd done. Her face would be sore, her stomach muscles would ache and her throat would be raw. Smiling, laughing and talking will do that to a body.

Chapter 11

Portia couldn't take it any longer. Viv's attorney, Mr. Henderson, wasn't taking her calls and she wanted information, and wanted it now. She sat in her car in the parking lot of the attorney's building. Portia had quit smoking five years ago, but this was a deal breaker. She lit her first cigarette in 60 months. Her eyes teared up. Her throat closed in on the smoke. Her nice pink lungs screamed. Coughing and hacking, she fought to get out of the car, she threw the butt to the pavement, and stomped it. Then the shot of nicotine sent her head buzzing. Dammit. She leaned against her car. Wow, can't smoke anymore I guess. As she pulled on the door handle, she spotted Henderson strolling into the parking lot, headed for his car. Portia jogged to his side.

"Portia!" He was not happy to see her. Henderson preferred his confrontations in the courtroom, with bailiffs and witnesses. He didn't even like to argue with his wife and kids.

"I know. I know. You can't tell me anything. But you stopped taking my calls, and I need to know something, anything. This not knowing is bringing out some weird, obsessive side in me."

"I see that. Portia, the best thing to do is to be patient. You've written her over and over. Give her some time."

"Will you at least tell me if she's all right?"

Henderson turned to her as he opened his car door. "I can't tell you anything."

"That's total bullshit. You can give me something that is not privileged information."

"I can't discuss anything with you. It would be like you talking about patients. Like that National Tab crap a few years ago."

That shot her down.

"Fine. At least tell me that my letters are getting to her."

"I place your letters in a box with other mail each quarter and send them to her. If they were in the box when it left my office, then one has to assume she has received your letters. Now, I must leave."

"Gee, thanks a million." Portia, crestfallen, started to slink away with her head down.

"And Portia?"

"Yes?"

"If you pull a stunt like this again…"

"I know, I know."

*   *   *   *   *

Coach Stromberg hadn't thought of putting heat on Viv's attorney, but when he followed Portia that day, as was his routine on Tuesdays and Thursdays, low and behold. She had a quickie meeting with the damn attorney in the parking lot. He put his binoculars down on the seat beside him and waited for Portia to pull out of the parking lot. He checked his notes. She would be off work until Saturday. She should be going home now. And since he had the code and the spare key to the condo, he would just apply some pressure to Portia.

Portia spent time crying and venting on her way home. "It's not right. It's more than not right, dammit, it's not fair." Her OB-GYN said she might be pre-menopausal and that would explain the mood swings. They were both waiting for the results of the saliva tests to determine the hormone levels in her system. That had to be it. "I'm hormonal, hormonal equals abnormal, they almost rhyme." Another crying jag. A slap or two of the steering wheel. Which didn't help much. She pulled in through the security gate with one thing on her mind. A tall glass- or several short ones of Pinot and a long, hot bath.

Stromberg waited in his car across the street from the condo. From his close observation a few weeks back, it was her pattern to come home on Thursdays, pour some wine, and disappear into the bathroom for at least an hour. This all started the first fifteen minutes of her arriving home. His spying techniques were anything but hi-tech, he simply took his dog for a walk and easily slipped past the gate, then let his dog loose. If he was ever stopped he would pretend that he was searching for his dog. Seven dog walking missions and he hadn't been stopped yet. It was easy to linger in front of the ground floor condo, leash in hand, and casually observe Portia through a front window.

Leash in hand, his alleged dog on the run somewhere in the condo complex. The faint beep on his wrist watch let him know that it had been nineteen minutes. Time enough for her to suck down some wine, fill up the tub, and slip into the water.

Stromberg turned his back to the front door and slowly, without any sudden action, back-stepped up the sidewalk until he could touch the doorknob with his hand behind his back. No one pulled through the parking lot. None of the tenants came outside. No curtains fluttered. He turned and, without a noise, slid the key home. Turning the knob, he eased the door open a half inch at a time. Finally, the door was open wide enough for him to enter. He could smell the aroma of a heavily scented candle. Some sort of classical music hummed from the bedroom. He inched his way through the bedroom, along a wall leading to the bathroom. His view was unobstructed into the bathroom. Portia lay in the warm water, her head tilted back against the edge of the tub. Four lit candles sat on the sink top. Damn classical music. Not to his liking. Portia was nearly asleep, awash in the warm water, the wine teasing at her tightness. He stepped across the bathroom floor and sat down on the toilet, glaring down at her.

"Now I want you to be very calm and

very quiet."

No sooner had the words oozed from his mouth than Portia shot straight up in the bathtub, screaming so loud it hurt his ears. First it was a full force horror movie scream, then it transmuted into help. Lastly, forcefully, it became "GET OUT!" All the while, he sat on the toilet, palms out, telling her to calm down and that nothing would happen to her.

"Nothing will happen to me!" Standing buck naked in the tub, soapy bubbles drying, popping, and sloughing off her glistening body, she looked around for a weapon, something to swing at him, or clobber the hell out of him with. The first thing she reached was a tall bottle of hair conditioner. She drew back and let it fly. He blocked it and it fell to the floor.

"We don't have to do this. I just want to talk to you about Vivika."

Her eyes went wild. Another round of screaming help and get out. The man wasn't leaving. She reached down and grabbed the matching shampoo bottle.

"C'mon Portia, tell me what you and Henderson talked about."

"You prick!!! You've been following me?" Her finger manipulated the lid on the shampoo, pulled it up to chest level and squeezed the bottle with all she had. A solid purple stream of shampoo hit the coach right between his black and blue eyes, both eyes filling with the sticky, stinging fluid. The more he wiped, the worse it got. His tear ducts added extra fluids, an involuntary action to aid in the flushing of a foreign body from the eyes. It didn't work. He rubbed hard and fast and little suds started to appear under his eyes.

He stumbled around the smallish bathroom. Portia burped the shampoo bottle, it gulped a refill of air and she squeezed it again, at his feet. A third of the shampoo had gone into his eyes. Most of the remaining two thirds went under his feet. She looked around for other fluids to add to the mix as he bounced into the wall, and the sink counter. Now it was his turn to scream. His screaming sounded more like a piglet, short bursts of screams, over and over. She spotted her bottle of light blue bath oil, snatched it up, and sprayed that on the floor. For good measure she pointed the stream up and down Stromberg, coating his body with a highly aromatic oil slick. Another bottle came out. Not remembering its purpose in her bathroom, Portia squirted heavy white goop over his slimy body.

"Will you stop!!" He figured out where the bathroom sink was, turned on the water, and was throwing handful after handful of water in his eyes.

Portia, warrior goddess of the lavatory, stepped from the tub, and using the grab bars that had been installed for Vivika's use, stabilized her footing. She took the toilet scrubber brush from its holder and slapped at his ear. She stuck it in his ear and twisted 'round and 'round like she was trying get a greasy hairball out of a clogged drain, then poked him in the neck and ribs, driving the semi-sharp end of the handle home to a target with each jab. She thrusted and parried, constantly finding another area of attack. The coach screamed out with each poke, but he refused to stop flushing his eyes. The small shelf above the toilet held a full bottle of Listerine mouthwash. She gingerly held on to the grab bar and reached out for the bottle. She opened it and poured the entire bottle on the coach's exposed head. The fine watery liquid ran off and into his eyes as fast it came out of the bottle.

He forced himself away from the water and out of the bathroom, falling to his knees as he desperately headed for the front door. As soon as his big body was out of the way, Portia hit her bedroom, pulled on her work scrubs, and went back into the other room for another attack.

"That bastard!" The front door was open and he was nowhere in sight. She ran out looking for him, watching the tracks of goo on the sidewalk until it vanished in the deep lush green grass of the condo complex.

"Son of a bitch!!!" She stood with her hands on her hips, looking around. There wasn't another soul in sight. Not a single person came to her aid. Either they were all watching the evening news, or all her neighbors were deaf. She hated them all.

Portia stood defiantly on the short sidewalk leading to her front door, daring the raccoon-faced freak to come back. It started as a nervous giggle, a relief it was over, and gratitude for her years of playing volleyball. She grinned and fought the giggle. Her street defense trainer would be proud of her. She lived up to his philosophy: Portia, there are no rules in a street fight. Never give up, and breathe! The grin gave way to a full blown laughing attack. She bent over at the waist and held herself. His eyes, his squealing! She would make damn sure that if there was a next time, she would be dressed for it and on solid ground.

Stromberg had two ridiculously black eyes from his run in with the man in black and now this. "That bitch Vivika will pay with her life for this. Enough of this shit. Henderson was the key. I tried to play nice with these people. Tried the PI. Got attacked by Portia the Amazon. I'll pay Henderson a visit after closing time." An amalgam of shampoo, conditioner, and a spittle of mouthwash rolled from his eyebrow down into the corner of his eye.

Chapter 12

"Where do we go for this Indiana Taco?" Vivika asked as Montez closed the car door for her.

"Indian, not Indiana." He chuckled.

"Oh that's right." She couldn't remember the last time she had felt this playful and flirty. Literally couldn't remember.

"Over in Elephant Butte. Right out there." He pointed out in the distance. She could make out a few roofs but little else.

"This is great. A personal tour guide and a free lunch." A tinge of embarrassment for being too playful brushed her cheeks.

"I thought you said we were going Dutch?" He smiled as he started the car and drove out of the hotel parking lot.

A short lived flat silence fell between them. "Now what?" She asked.

"How about the basics?"

"For instance?"

"Hmm, my name is BJ Montez. I'm a highway patrolman. I'm twenty-nine, born about eighty miles from here. I like long walks in the desert, puppies, kittens, fishing and sunsets." He was proud of his charming dissertation.

She reached her hand out for a handshake. "My name is Vivika Stryker, I like Slurpees, corn nuts, small towns in the desert, cops, and hopefully Indiana Tacos."

Montez laughed as he drove the few short miles from Truth or Consequences to Elephant Butte, "A little music?"

"Sure."

He reached over to the radio, turned it up real loud, and then punched the mute button. "There ya go." He looked at her. She had a blank expression on her face like he was nuts. Then they both cracked up and laughed at his little joke.

"You're a comedian and a cop?" She asked, with a little laugh in her voice.

"Is it that obvious?" They both chuckled.

She reached and turned the tunes back on. Country music drifted out from the speakers. It wasn't what she listened to, but it fit the mood and occasion. The singer with a deep, gravely-- nasally voice sang that he was the only daddy that would walk the line.

"Oh I like this guy's voice. What's his name?"

Mostly shocked, but understanding that she was from Seattle, not exactly a haven of country music, and maybe she never listened to Waylon Jennings, being tied to her practice in a gym for the last twelve years.

"Vivika, that's Waylon Jennings. You've never heard of him?"

"Apparently not. I'd remember a voice and a song like that."

Montez motored down into a shallow canyon, and eventually up and out the other end, coming to a stop sign. "Almost there."

"No hurry. This song is nice too." Apparently she liked Conway Twitty as well. She harmonized, "So don't call him a cowboy until you've seen him ride." She embarrassed herself, blushing as she stared out the window. The oddities of the desert outside made her ponder why someone would have a forty-foot sailboat for sale. Very optimistic indeed. As he drove, Vivika noticed three or four boat storage facilities, and lots of mobile homes perched on top of what she thought were sand dunes. And a golf course. In the desert?

Vivika reminded him of his baby sister. Just a girl being a girl, singing along with the radio, looking bored, staring out the window.

Montez came to another stop sign at a T intersection, and then made a left. Vivika counted three gas stations, one taqureia, two more boat storage businesses plus four RV campgrounds. "Officer Montez, what's with all the damn boats?"

"Boats? Oh, there's a lake right out there."

She, being preoccupied with the terrain directly out the window, hadn't noticed the crystal blue lake past the roof line of the little town they pulled into. "Wow!"

"Elephant Butte Lake. It's pretty and clear, no wind whipping it around. We can drive down there after lunch if you want?"

"Heck yeah, it looks great from here."

"We're here."

Here was painted salmon pink and turquoise with some strange Native American symbols emblazoned on the walls. The building was a low slung but proud looking adobe. The parking lot was gravel and loud under the tires. A black lettered sign welcomed them: "Momma's Table -- Authentic Mexican and Native Fare."

Inside the eatery, several locals sat around colorfully covered tables in mix and match chairs. The floor was large red tiles. And the aroma was intoxicating.

"C'mon." He turned and motioned for her. She followed him straight into the kitchen. A short, round woman with a white apron threw her arms around Montez. "Mom, this is Vivika Stryker. She's visiting from Seattle."

"Oh it's so nice to meet you, Miss Stryker." His mother said.

"Please, call me Viv."

"And you call me Momma." Unable to hide her cherubic broad smile, Montez's mom wrapped her arms around Viv as if she were a long lost family member.

"You kids hungry?" Momma asked.

"Of course. Why else would I show up?" Montez joked. Momma slugged him in the arm.

"Momma, he's been bragging all day about your Indiana tacos." She shot a wink toward Montez.

"No honey, they are called Indian tacos."

"She knows what they are called,

Momma. She's just joking with *me!*"

"Okay, you two go sit. I'll bring you your plates in a few minutes." Momma hustled back to her orders in waiting.

Montez showed Vivika out to the dining room, picked out a table for them, and asked her about drinks. Whatever you're having was her answer. He went to the drink fountain across the floor on another wall, poured two iced teas, and came back to the table.

"This place is so cute." She swung around in her chair to admire the eclectic items collected and displayed along the walls.

"They've put a lot of work into this place. All of us kids have worked on it with them. I painted all of the window frames. My sister helped hang the light fixtures."

"A family project?"

"Yep. Mom and Dad used to have a station wagon with a little trailer and they would go to rodeos, football games, flea markets, and whatever with that little trailer and all of us kids in the back end of the of the station wagon. We'd all help cook the tacos out of that little trailer."

"Sounds boring for little kids."

"It was at times. I'd walk around the event with a taco all over my face, moaning about how good it was. People would stop me and ask me where I got it. So I'd tell them!" He chuckled.

"What do they call that? Oh yeah, a shill!" She giggled. Vivika wondered why she knew that word.

"It worked. I helped increase sales wherever we went."

"So, you're just increasing sales again today? How do I know these things are really good?"

"You won't have to wait long. Here comes Momma."

Momma was carrying two industrial strength platters, piled high with goodness.

"Be careful, sweetie. These plates are hot." Momma warned as she scooted the plates onto the table, arranging them in front of her two guests.

"Wow!" Vivika was bowled over with the size of the serving.

"Nice huh?" Montez smiled as he watched her figuring out her angle of attack.

"So what is this exactly?" She studied the seemingly endless pile of food stacked on the plate.

"It starts with fry bread, called an Indian tortilla, handmade, freshly cooked. That's the foundation of any Indian taco. Then you add anything you want. Cheese, meat of any kind, lettuce, peppers, whatever you want on it." He admired a healthy appetite. It would be a pleasure watching her eat.

"Hands or knife and fork?" She quizzed him.

"I use a knife and fork, but a lot of people just pick it up and eat it. Some fold it in half. Six of one, thirteen dozen of the other." He motioned for her to try it first.

She cut off a piece, scooped it up with her fork and took a mouthful of the most delicious food she could remember. "Oh my god, this is great!" She chewed, talked, and wiped her mouth in one motion.

"Better than corn nuts?" He laughed.

"Don't push it! Hell yes, better than corn nuts. What kind of meat is this?"

"Shredded roast buffalo. Momma adds her own blend of spices."

Another bite gobbled up. "Oh, this is so good!"

He nibbled at his taco as he enjoyed watching her chow down.

She fell silent and took charge of the platter. Cut, scoop, chew, and smile. After a few minutes, she was down to just a few pieces of grated cheese, buffalo meat crumbs, and lettuce. She grabbed a tortilla chip from a bowl on the table and used it as a miniature shovel, chasing all the little remnants around until they sat on the chip, then devouring chip and all.

Montez sat back in his chair, having finished his taco several minutes before she did and enjoyed the show.

"Wow that was soooooooo good!" She took a sip of iced tea. "I love Indiana tacos!!" She said.

"Sheeesh, now you just need to call them by their rightful name." Montez reached over and patted her forearm. He chuckled.

Momma quietly walked up to the table from the kitchen, where she had watched them both eat. "Are you kids ready for dessert?" She stood at the corner of the table between them, looking intently at Vivika, but glancing at her son as well. "Mom, I'm not sure I can…"

"Heck yeah Momma, I'm ready."

Momma laid her hand on Vivika's shoulder, squeezed, and walked away.

"You sure you can eat dessert?" He looked at her as she rubbed her tummy with both hands.

"Not a problem. Apparently I'm a big eater." She smiled over the lip of the glass of iced tea as she took a swallow of the cold liquid.

"Ok, we can stop and get you some Pepto."

"Here you go." Momma returned with another platter sized plate. In the center she'd placed six mini-tarts, and surrounding the centerpiece, two inch long twisted bread sticks coated with cinnamon and sprinkled with sugar. "I've been experimenting with caramelized peach tarts. The peaches came from old Marv's backyard."

"Be careful Viv. When mom experiments, things get weird."

Momma playful slapped her son's shoulder. "Don't poison the young lady's mind against me."

Vivika took a small tart. One bite and half, the tart vanished. "Hmmmmmm! Wow!"

She dropped the rest of the tart on her tongue and let out another yummy sound. "These are great!" She reached for another one.

Montez took one and ate the entire tart with one bite. "Not bad, Mom."

"I'm so glad you like them, Vivika. Ok, Billy, time for you to bus this table and do the dishes. C'mon..." She tugged at his shirt collar. "I'm taking my break early, to talk to Vivika."

"Yes Billy, go do the dishes." Vivika chimed in with a wink.

He started to give his mother some attitude. "Go on now, shoo." She snapped a white dish towel, finding home on his left butt cheek. He jumped and let out a howl.

"Boys, what can you do with them?" Momma took her son's chair and closed the gap slightly between her and Vivika.

"What can you do?" Vivika took Momma's side. She could hear dishes clattering in the kitchen.

"So, how long have you two been secretly dating?" Momma stared intently waiting for Vivika's answer.

"Dating?"

"He never brings his girlfriends here for the first month, so, how long?"

"Let's see. Counting today?"

Momma's expression was as if she was waiting for the last two lottery numbers to be read. "Yes, counting today."

Viv leaned into Momma, "This is our first

date. I only met your son day before yesterday."

Momma's lottery ticket matched the last two numbers. "Oh my goodness." She reached out with both arms and bear hugged Vivika into submission. "Welcome to the family, sweetie."

"What? Wait!"

Momma let go of the hug and ran for the kitchen. "Billy! I'm so happy for you two!"

Vivika was on Momma's heels.

"Happy for who? For what?" Billy wiped the soap suds from his hands.

"Vivika just told me this is your first date, and you brought her here. Oh Billy I'm so happy for you!" She gave him a sloppy motherly kiss and a hug. She turned away crying, dabbing at the tears with the deadly accurate dish towel. "I have to go tell your father." She whisked her way out the back door of the restaurant to her husband's workshop in the back lot.

"What the hell was that all about?" Vivika asked.

"She wants grandchildren. And usually I don't bring my dates around here because she's... ummm."

"A mother who wants grandchildren?" Vivika finished his sentence.

"But really, really bad. More like obsessed." He added.

"I think she's wonderful."

"Hell of a cook, huh, kid?" Grumpy voice asked.

He turned back to the stainless steel tank

and continued washing dishes. "I almost didn't bring you here." Downcast, his mood changed.

"I don't see the problem."

"It's ok. I'll finish these up and we can go see the lake."

"Fine." She sensed the mood change and agreed quietly.

"Dahling... you know how I love the shore."

"I know."

"Pardon?"

"Hmm, I know it will be fine is all."

Chapter 13

"What's good for the pervert..." Portia sat in her car with binoculars pinpointed on Coach Stromberg as he walked out of his house toward his car. "Where are you heading now, Rocky Raccoon?" She'd gotten his home address from someone at the gym and for the third day in a row, she sat across the street and watched her prey. His rambling was mundane: a trip to the grocery store, a bar, a strip joint, the gym, gas station, and two passes through attorney Henderson's parking lot, and back to the gym.

A light drizzle fell without warning blurring the window she was looking out of. Stromberg's car passed her, she checked her gas gauge for the eighth or ninth time. She pulled out behind him, pacing him, but keeping a good distance between them. After fifteen minutes of stop and go traffic, she recognized the parking lot from the first night. He was back at the strip club. Such a perv. She pulled in and parked at the farthest space but could still see the front entrance and where he had parked his car. Portia glanced at the clock on the radio: 9:20. He would be in the club for an hour. She nestled into her seat and waited.

The combination of drizzle and the music on the radio caused a shallow streak of melancholy and drowsiness. Two blaring car horns jolted her awake. The time jumped to

11:15.

"Dammit!" She was fretful he had gotten his jollies and left while she dozed. She twisted on her wipers, clearing the windshield so she could see. One of the loud horns belonged to the Coach's car. He must have backed out and almost hit someone, as they were coming in the parking lot. Two men, one of which she was sure was Stromberg, were yelling at each other, flipping the bird and honking. Stromberg peeled out and sped past her. "Gotcha perv."

He swerved in and out of traffic. She lost him at one intersection and caught up to him three blocks later. He drove like a crazy person. Some stripper must have turned his tip down. She giggled at the mental picture. Rocky the perv was turned down.

The drizzle turned to an honest to god rain. She turned her wipers on high to keep up with the watershed. "Where are we going Rocky?" The street was familiar, even in the dark with it raining. He pulled into Henderson's parking lot. "He's going to break in to his office!" She pulled to the curb just outside the parking lot behind a large hedge. Instinctively she reached for her cell phone.

"Wait a minute." She calmed herself. "If I call this in, he gets busted. I know what he's going in there for, and I want the same thing. Viv's whereabouts." She struggled with the moral dilemma. He was out of sight. "It's an attorney's office; they have to have great security right?"

She sat with one hand in a death grip on the steering wheel, while the other hand held the cell phone. "I can always report him tomorrow?" She relaxed her hands. The cell phone went back to its place in the console. She waited.

Twenty minutes later, Stromberg slinked his way between the building and the parking lot, and made it to his car, with Portia on his tail.

Coach Stromberg drove straight home, stopping for each red light and stop sign, even using his turn signal. Didn't want to give the cops any reason to stop him. Once home, he got out of his car and walked into his house with a briefcase in hand, just another welcome home evening, albeit later than usual for his return home from the gym.

Portia exited her car and walked across the street. In front of his driveway, she bent down, pretending to tie her shoe. She casually looked in all directions as she ran the rabbit around the tree and into the hole. The coast was clear as far as she could tell. She took her time moving up the driveway to the Coach's house. Portia headed for the front door, and then faded off the sidewalk, across a short section of landscaping, and up to the front window to take a peek inside. Stromberg sat on the couch, the briefcase he carried into the house on a coffee table in front of him. He was scrutinizing a file. The same file Portia surmised she wanted to be reading and had wanted to read for many months. She had to have the file.

Portia left the front porch and walked around to the side of the house, looking for a gate. She found it, but the latch was out of alignment with the gate posts. She tinkered and jiggled the latch until finally the gate opened, about two inches, then the sagging gate sounded off on the concrete. Dammit. It was loud. He should have heard that. She held her breath in the dark, waiting, knowing any second the perv could be on her. But, he must have not heard the wood on concrete cat fight. She moved the gate open, slowly, cautiously.

She crept around the side of the house and tip-toed to the back. She found a sliding glass door that lead into the kitchen. Stromberg's head bobbed up and down as he shifted, reading the file and possibly taking notes. Think, Portia, think. She looked around on the semi-lit patio for inspiration. Typical patio furniture. A coiled garden hose. And recycling bins, filled with paper, plastics, aluminum cans and the glass bin full of liquor bottles. "I wonder." She walked out to the edge of the patio next to the grass. She could still see his head and shoulders where he sat on the couch. Another few feet past him, his car sat in the driveway. "Wonder if I can chuck a bottle over the roof to his car. He'd hear that, run out the front door. I run in the back door, snatch the file, run back out here... he'd run back in the house to call... who ... the cops? Not likely. Maybe he'd run back in the house for a gun? Shit." She stepped back over to the sliding glass door. The glass portion was wide open, the screen door was closed. Delicately, she tried the screen slider. It moved. It was unlocked. Back to the glass recycle bin. She selected two large clear bottles off the top of the bin. She took a whiff, vodka. She moved in the darkness out to the grass, holding the bottle by the neck, she guessed how much power to put in the throw. She cocked her arm and let the first one fly, and moved back to the patio. Silence. The bottle must have fallen on the grass in the front yard.

While she watched from the dark, Stromberg stood up, did something she couldn't see, and walked away from the couch. He was carrying the briefcase. Shit! He walked directly at her, and then made a sudden left into the kitchen. He set the briefcase down within a few feet of the sliding screen door. Stromberg took a glass from the dish drainer, grabbed some ice, and poured himself a drink, emptying the bottle. He took a gulp of the highball and walked to the slider, brought the bottle outside and placed it on the top of the glass recycling bin. He stepped to the edge of the patio, looked to the heavens for an empirical weather report. Still drippy weather. Go figure, it's Seattle. He went back inside, closing both the screen door and the glass door, picked up the drink, turned off the lights and sat back down on the couch.

Portia watched, crouched down behind the huge central heating unit just off the patio. She went back over to the recycling bin, took four bottles, crept back out to the grass and, in rapid succession, threw all four bottles over the house. She could tell by the sound the first bottle thumped the top of the roof, and then splattered on the driveway, the next three hit his car. It sounded wonderful to her. As the third bottle was still shattering, Coach Stromberg jumped up from the couch, ran to the front door where he grabbed a baseball bat standing guard, and charged out the front door to investigate the racket outside. He closed the door behind him.

As soon as he was off of the couch, Portia was in action, moving forward to the sliding glass patio door. The front door closed as she was opening the back door. She made sweet contact with the handle on the briefcase. It was hers now. She backed out the door, closing it, and strode into the dark, drippy night.

She watched and as he came back in the front door, she ran around the side of the house, making sure not to touch the loud gate. She sprinted to her car, hopped in, and snuck away from the scene.

Portia congratulated herself and stroked the top of the briefcase. "I know he didn't follow me, but just to be on the safe side." She took a leisurely circuitous route back to the condo, forty minutes worth of left turns, right turns, and circling the complex three times, making sure no one was following her.

She parked in her space in front of the condo, taking her time getting out of the car. No hurry, she wasn't doing anything other than coming home late. The briefcase tagged along with her as if she carried it everyday. She closed the door, locked the bolt, and leaned hard up against the door. Taking a deep cleansing breath, she let it out slow, just like she taught her patients to do. Giddy with her ninja results, Portia placed the briefcase on her bed and sat down beside it. The gold colored latches popped right open. The perv didn't lock them. Feeling like she was in some old pirate movie where the good guys finally got the treasure chest, she opened the lid and looked down into an empty briefcase. Totally barren, not even a pen or pencil in the little holders. Zero, zip, nada. Nothing but the stench of old cigars.

Portia collapsed into a pillow and screamed. "Nooooooo!

* * * * *

Coach Stromberg, bat in hand, stood in his driveway, looking at the carnage done to his car. A shattered windshield, broken bottles encircling his car. "Damn kids!" He walked around the car, taking inventory of what would need to be fixed or replaced. "Dammit."

He lingered for a few more minutes, and then walked back in the house, sat down, continuing to read up on Vivika's whereabouts. The file just where he left it.

Chapter 14

Following her ninja antics, Portia called in sick the next morning. All she wanted was her bed, and comfort food.

Attorney Henderson was shocked when he arrived at his office. The door was kicked in, and a locked file cabinet had been pried open. The file drawer holding the letters SHO to STU was pulled all the way out. Instantly he knew the file of Stryker, Vivika, would be missing. Not the petty cash, not the computers and other electronics.

Two hours after he called in the complaint of his office being burglarized, the police officer had one last question for the good attorney. "Do you have any thoughts as to who would want that file?"

"Yes. Portia Connely. Here's her full name, address, phone number, and where she works."

*　　*　　*　　*　　*

Portia had barely finished her main comfort food for the day, mac and cheese, and crawled back in bed when the door bell rang. "Dammit."

She checked the peephole. "Shit, it's the police." Every possible thought criss-crossed her synapses. They knocked on the door again.

She opened the door with her best "I just woke up" smile. "Can I help you officer?"

"Portia Connely?"

"Yes. Is there something wrong?"

"We need to ask you a few questions. You'll need to come with us downtown…"

*   *   *   *   *

"What in the hell did I do with that briefcase?" Coach Stromberg checked every room in his house. Under the kitchen sink. The garage. His car. Just for the hell of it, since he had taken another empty outside to the recycle bin, what the hell, maybe he took it with him, so he checked outside near the recycle bins. "I know I had that thing last night." He turned to go back in his house and spotted the muddy footprints on the patio. Footprints coming from the side of the house, across the patio, up to the sliding glass door, then out to the grass and back again. "Dammit, how many people were back here?" The footprints were everywhere on the concrete patio. The drizzly, drippy night made perfect conditions for shoes to pick up mud from the front flowerbeds and the muddy patch by the central heating unit. He stood there scratching his head, counting the steps, with a growing hunch that whoever made the prints took the briefcase. But those damn kids tearing up his car, that, that really pissed him off.

*   *   *   *   *

Everything in the world ran through Portia's mind. "How did he figure out it was me? Fingerprints on the bottles? On the sliding glass door? Witnesses? It would only be vandalism, except for the breaking and entering. Misdemeanor or felony? Fine or jail time?"

"Can I put some clothes on?" She asked the officer patiently waiting two feet from her, not taking his eyes off of her.

"Sure, but hurry up. And leave the door open."

Leave the door open? "Oh, right, in case I have weapons?"

"Do you?" He asked.

"Of course not. I'll be right back." On her way across the living room to her bedroom, she passed by the briefcase on the coffee table. Shit. Might as well confess and be done with it.

She pulled on a pair of jeans, a dark purple sweater, shoes, and grabbed her pocket book on the way out the door with her uniformed escort.

She had never been in the backseat of a cop car before. It was cramped and had a heavy odor of spray can sanitizer, but was cleaner than a New York cab. Portia watched the neighborhoods through the security screen. The radio chatter on the officer in-car radio was interesting, but they were speaking a foreign language. "1087 clear. RO in en route. NCIC (National Crime

Information Center) clear, no wants or warrants." The voices on the air changed, as did the content and urgency in the tone of their voices.

It didn't take the officer long to buzz through traffic and arrive at the station. After she tried to open the door from the inside, he opened the door for her and took her by the elbow into the station. He signed her in at the front desk, and then led her down a hallway and she waited in a non-descript room with bold letters on the door, Interview 1. She kept waiting for some TV cop show theme music to filter into the room. There was no two-way mirror, a small, hidden video camera made up the difference. Maybe Vincent D'Onofrio would barge in the room at any second and try and trick her into a confession. Instead, in walked an overweight, tall man with a white Ernest Hemmingway look-a-like beard.

"Good morning." He carried a thin manila file folder and a cup of coffee.

"Good morning." What was she supposed to say?

"Want some coffee or something?" He asked.

"No thanks. Why am I here this morning?"

"You tell me."

"Tell you what?" She asked as he sat down across from her at the table.

"Let's start with where you were last night between, oh let's say between eight and midnight?"

"After work, I, I stopped for a bite to eat. Stopped at the drug store for some personal items." She watched him taking notes on a slip of paper in the file.

"After the drug store where did you go?"

"Home. Had some wine and a hot bath, and then went to bed around 10:30."

"And how long were you in Mr. Henderson's office?"

"What?"

"Look Miss Connely, Henderson doesn't want to press charges. He just wants the files and briefcase back."

"What files? What briefcase? I wasn't in his office last night. I talked to him in the parking lot the other day, but he refused..."

"So you were pissed off and broke into his office to get the information he wouldn't give you."

"He's making this shit up. I never broke into his office!"

"Fine. Just so you know, even though he looks like a harmless pharmacist, the man is fairly powerful around town. He has a lot of friends in this department. He doesn't want to press charges, but he has asked us to look into this as a favor to him."

"Okay, but that doesn't change the fact that I didn't break into his office."

Hemmingway looked down at the file and read off the make, model, and license plate number of her car, the name of the rehab facility where she worked, the address, phone number, her boss's name. The shift she was working. "You broke into his office. That alone is not a huge crime." He looked back at the file. "The files and briefcase only come up to a class three felony. Basically, a fine and probation. But the damage to the door, the fifteen hundred bucks in petty cash that you took, pushes this to a class one felony. Fines, restitution, minimum one year in county lock up."

"Petty cash? Are you on drugs? I didn't break into his office."

A knock at the door interrupted the interrogation. "Come in." The officer that picked her up came in, whispered something in Hemmingway's ear. "Fine."

"Miss Connely, I have no choice."

His words rocked her to the core.

"I'm going to let you go at this point and start a formal investigation. You might want to get an attorney. But knowing Henderson the way I do, you'll have to find one out of town. No attorney that wants to keep working in Seattle will touch you or your case."

"But this isn't fair!"

"Fair?" He stood up. "You'll need to call a cab for a ride home."

"What? You pricks brought me down here!"

"That is where the fair part stopped." He took the file off the table. He could hear her begin to cry. He looked back. She had her face buried in her hands. "Remember, Miss Connely, he doesn't want to press charges." He was between the table and the door when he turned one last time. "Where's the briefcase?"

"On my coffee..." Shit.

*   *   *   *   *

Flush with new information, Coach Stromberg checked the web for an airline ticket to New Mexico. Without making reservations a minimum of two weeks in advance, the ticket prices were outside his dwindling budget. $700, $680, $822, round trip to Albuquerque, with a connection to Las Cruces. A rental car. Hotel. He was damn near broke and his one legged wife had all of the money. No choice but to drive his car, sleep in it, rough it down there. Once he got his hands around the bitch's neck, he could fly anywhere first class. He'd choke the money out of her if she wanted it that way.

He inhaled another shot of vodka, sitting there on his couch studying the file on his wife. The receipt for the overnight mail was on top of the paperwork. The date was less than a week old. Overnight package, 30 lbs, Desert View Motel, Truth or Consequences, New Mexico. He reached for the half full bottle instead of the glass, and knocked back two mouthfuls. "Game set match little Vivika." Stromberg stood up to take his first shower in three days and the vodka he'd been guzzling all morning rushed through his system and slammed into his brain. Lights out. He didn't even feel the hard floor when he crashed face first next to his favorite couch. A new chipped tooth to go along with the broken nose and raccoon eyes.

*   *   *   *   *

"Coffee what? What was that?" Hemmingway came back to the table.

"Fine. You caught me. But you'll be as disappointed as I am."

"How's that?" Pen in hand, taking notes.

"Yes I had a run-in with Henderson. The prick wouldn't tell me anything about Vivika. After work I had a couple glasses of wine for courage. I drove back over to his office about nine, sat in the parking lot, working up my nerve. I went up to his office, tried the door knob, and pushed hard on the door. It wouldn't budge. Then I heard someone walking toward me. I jumped across the breezeway and hid. This wiry guy, shorter than me, walks up to Henderson's door, kicks the door about five or six times before it opened. In he goes."

"And you're standing a few feet away watching from the dark?"

"Yes."

"Okay, keep going."

"In he goes. He's got a small penlight or something. I can see everything he's doing. He goes to a long bank of file cabinets. Opens one up, pulls a file out, looks around the office with his light, picks up a briefcase on the floor next to the desk. Sneaks back to the door, looks both ways down the breezeway, and steps out. And walks away like nothing happened."

"What did he look like?"

"Shorter than me. Black or dark blue hoodie, same for the sweat pants."

"What did you do when he left the office?"

"Honestly, I didn't know what to do. The little bastard beat me to it. I went into the office. I had a small flashlight. I went to the file cabinets, noticed the drawer where Vivika's file should be, and it was open. I pulled it all the way out. Her file was gone."

"You actually want me to believe this shit?" Hemmingway said looking her in the eye.

"Look. What do I have to lose at this point? So I ran out of the office, and there was a car leaving the parking lot."

"What did it look like?"

"Like every other one of these boom box fart can exhaust cars on the road. Low to the ground, loud exhaust."

"What color was it?"

"Could have been brown or bronze. I know it wasn't black or red or blue."

"Fine. We have an unidentified male in an unidentifiable car with loud exhaust."

"I didn't know I was supposed to take notes while committing a crime!"

"Fine. What did you do next?"

"I ran straight for my car and I followed him the best I could. I lost him a couple of times, and just when I was about to give up, he came out of a gas station by the airport. I couldn't believe it. I followed him for another few minutes. He pulled into a strip club. I pulled in behind him and parked where I could watch him. Another guy approached his car."

"Don't tell me, it was the Tin Man, but he was painted black."

"No. This guy had on a warm up suit. Bright white strips on the shoulders, down the chest. His shoes had that reflector tape on the soles and when he turned away from me, some headlights shined on the name on the back. Tyson or Tri-State, something like that."

"It was Tyson or Tri something?"

"The material wasn't perfectly flat and it only flashed for a few seconds."

"Fine. Do you remember the name of the strip club?"

"Parkers? Over by the airport."

"At least that's something. Then what?"

"The guy in the warm up suit walked up to the short guy in the car. He got out of the car. They hugged."

"They hugged?"

"You know, like a street hug or when football players greet each other. Quick, a fist on the back, that sort of hug."

"Gotcha. Then?"

"The short one in the black hoodie handed the other guy the briefcase. They turned and walked over to the other guy's car. And then they went into the club together."

"And then what happened?"

"I got out of my car and snuck between the cars, looked in the other guy's car. The briefcase was right on the front seat. I tried the door, and it opened, so I reached in and snatched it. And ran as fast as I could back to my car and drove like a crazy person back to my condo."

"No one saw you? No one followed you?"

"Nope, I made sure of that. I get home, open the briefcase, and the son of a bitch was empty. No files, pens... nothing!"

"And you still have the briefcase?" Earlier when the officer whispered in his ear, he informed Hemmingway he saw a briefcase on her coffee table.

"Yes. Take it and check it for fingerprints! Maybe the kid and the other guy left fingerprints on it!" She commanded.

"Let me have the officer take you home and I'll have him pick it up. Is there anything else you can or will tell me?"

"That's all I've got. I swiped the briefcase from the guy that broke into the office and it's empty and you're welcome to it."

"One last question."

"Go for it." She was free and clear, that much she was sure of.

"What's your interest in this," He flipped

his note pad back a few pages, "Vivika Stryker?"

"She was a patient of mine, and we became..." She hesitated.

"Lovers?"

"*OH GOD NO!*" Portia burst out in laughter. "We became close friends. Sold me her condo. Left town, and I haven't heard from her since. All I can do is write letters to her, send them to tight ass Henderson, and he forwards them."

"Friends huh?"

"Yes. Close friends."

He stood up, opened the door and spoke to the officer waiting there. "Ok, Miss Connely we're done for now. Officer Jantz will take you home and pick up the briefcase. I'll be in touch." He disappeared down the hallway.

Chapter 15

"Robert, don't start!" Momma scolded as she walked a half a step behind her husband. They were coming out of the front door of the café. "Robert *be* nice."

Robert Montez had his sights set on the short woman standing next to his son.

"So this is *your* Vivika." He took Vivika's hand, holding it, light as a caress. He stepped back to check her out, head to toe. Then, slowly, he stepped back in, raised her hand, and kissed the back of it. "Welcome to New Mexico, Miss Stryker."

She looked to Montez for guidance. All he could do was roll his eyes and look skyward. "Mom!"

"Ok, Robert, knock it off. You'll scare the poor thing." She playfully slapped him on the back of his lecherous hand.

Vivika, naturally, wasn't sure how to respond. If only she had half of her memory back, then she would have a pat response for sure. But a perfect stranger kissing the back of your hand? And his voice was deeply familiar. That memory thing again.

"It's nice to meet you too, Robert." She didn't know why or what it was called, but she pulled a half curtsy from somewhere.

"Please, call me Bob. Dad would be better." He smiled, still holding her hand.

"Ok Dad." She flashed a big toothy grin. If you can't beat'em, join'em. Vivika played along, at least until she felt comfortable with the attention.

"Come, sit. Let's have some iced tea and talk." Robert, Bob, Dad said.

"Dad we just finished lunch, we're stuffed. I'm taking Vivika for the grand tour of the lake. We need to go." Montez pleaded with his father.

"Then you *must* come back for dinner. Right Momma?" Robert asked his wife without taking his cool dark gray eyes from Vivika's.

"By all means. I insist!" Momma had spoken. She glared at her son, daring him to say no.

Sensing her testiness and not wanting to take her on, he passed it off, "Viv, what do you think? Wanna come back for dinner?" He hoped she'd say no, so the evening would be just the two of them.

"I would love to!" Her words still on the air, Robert reacted and she went with it, accepting a hug from him. He lifted her off her feet and spun her around.

"You can eat here anytime, and *don't* ever have to wash dishes for your supper." Robert, Bob, Dad declared.

"That's quite an offer for someone who doesn't do dishes himself!" Momma chided him. "C'mon Robert, we have to get ready for dinner service."

"See you soon." Dad winked at Vivika. "And you too son." He shot him a different kind of wink.

Montez opened the car door for Vivika. As he did, he apologized. "I've never seen them like this."

She sat down in the seat. "It's fine. I love them already."

He shook his head. Soon enough he would be out of his parents' parking lot and heading toward the lake, only to be forced to come back later in the evening for another performance.

"Wow, what great parents you have!" Vivika meant every word.

"They can be a handful, but they mean well."

"I wish I could remember who your Dad reminds me of."

"Which part?" He chuckled.

"His voice I think."

"Oh, that's easy. Ricardo Montalban."

"Who?"

"The suave, slick-voiced host of Fantasy Island. The old TV show."

"If you say so." God, if she could only remember.

"He gets that a lot from the tourists. Sometimes he'll greet people at the door and really turn the schmooz on."

"You mean that was Dad turned down on low?" She laughed aloud.

"Yep." With one eye on the road, he broke into a gentle dissertation on his parents. He had seen his parents at their best and worst. The lean years in the station wagon, his Dad's drinking and disappearing for a few days here and there, catching up to mom and the kids on the road at the next rodeo, football game or flea market. His Dad always seemed to find them. From New Mexico to Colorado, Southern Texas to Arizona, his old man always showed up. At their best, they could be nauseating. The last few minutes were the perfect example. Happy and flush with cash, the café was going strong and sustainable, with locals and tourists. He couldn't be prouder or happier for them. His parents were proud of all their kids. BJ gave a resume' of each sibling. Sister Lou was studying marine biology in graduate school. Les, his oldest brother was a captain in the Air Force, currently on some secret base somewhere in the Middle East. Bob, Jr., went through a rough patch. For a while he was the poster child for the song, 'I fight authority…', but he's married, has a young son, lives in Missouri, and is a district manager for a home improvement store." And himself, BA in criminal law, five years as a highway patrol officer.

"From living in a station wagon to a total family success story. Wow."

Montez drove up to the park ranger booth and checked in with the ranger on duty. The ranger waved him on through the gate. He followed the park road down to the water's edge, parked and they both got out. They walked a half hour in one direction, turned and walked back to the start. They walked a half hour in the other direction.

As they approached the car, "I've got an idea. Let's go." Montez said. Back in the car, he made a u-turn and headed back up the park road, just before the ranger's station, he turned onto a dirt road and stopped in front of a closed gate that warned, "Authorized Vehicles Only". He stepped out, and opened the closed gate.

"Officer Montez, are you driving an authorized vehicle?" He could hear the smile in her voice.

"Yes, ma'am." He pulled a short distance past the gate, and then stepped out to close it. He proceeded on the dirt road.

"Kind of bumpy isn't it?" She commented.

"It's been worse."

To Vivika it seemed like he drove forever without getting very far from the gate. Not much to see, up a hill, around a sharp corner, down, and then back up. She finally lost sight of the gate and the lake.

"Is this where you dump the bodies?" She jokingly asked.

"Just a few more minutes, I promise."

And it was, just a few more minutes. They came to a stop on a flat spot. They were higher than the surrounding terrain.

"C'mon." He got out of the car.

She got out of the car and followed him several feet in front of the car. The ground fell away. It was a vista point the rangers used to keep an eye on campers, boaters, and poachers. It also served as a crow's nest to look for missing hikers.

The lake was so far away it looked like an oversized pond. The gate they passed through was barely visible.

"This is incredible!" Vivika was impressed at Montez's secluded viewing area.

"I like to come here on my days off. And I really like coming up here during the meteor showers. You wouldn't believe what they look like from here."

She took in the breathtaking beauty below her. The azure shoreline of Elephant Butte Lake was stunning. She could make out a huge V rolling across the lake, the wake of a boat. At this distance, it was shimmering artwork.

"So you like?" He said grinning.

"Officer Montez,"

"You really can start calling me Billy or Bill now."

"Billy, I honestly don't remember seeing anything like this. Yes, I really love it up here."

"I have a blanket in the trunk if you want to just sit. Look, and listen for a bit. We have another two hours before they'll start sending out a search party."

"Who, the rangers?"

"No, Mom and Dad!" He laughed.

"They would, wouldn't they?" She laughed. "Sure, grab the blanket. I'll sit here for a little while."

"Dahling, a blanket, a man, under the stars, I like the new you."

"I think I do too."

"Pardon?"

"Oh nothing, just thinking out loud."

The two sat in silence save for a quick "oh look over there" for two hours. The sun dropped behind the western mountains, leaving plenty of orange and golden rays filling the sky.

"Lay back." Billy checked his watch.

"Excuse me?" A little off guard.

"No seriously, you can only see it if you lay back."

Vivika did as she was asked. She waited for some kind of move on his part, but he lay still, only an inch from her.

He pointed up and to his left. "Now watch riiiight up there." As the words came out, a bright yellow ball came into sight and moved right over them. Several hundred miles overhead, a satellite on its orbit crossed their path.

"Oh my goodness what is that? A UFO?"

"It's a satellite silly. You've never seen one passing over?"

"Apparently not. It's neat. Oh it's gone already?"

"They're moving pretty fast. So you have to match the sun, their trajectory. Everything has to line up. I've even spotted the space shuttle a few of times."

"Wow, I'd like to see that!" Vivika decided laying a blanket, in the desert at sunset was very comfortable.

"I like it too kid." Grumpy added his two cents.

"I'm sure you do."

"Do what?" Billy asked.

"Pardon me?"

"You said, 'I'm sure you do'."

"Oh, I was thinking you probably really like being up here and seeing all of this." She stood. "I need to use the little girls' room."

"Not a problem." He dusted the blanket off, tossed it back in the trunk, and they drove back down the dirt road. "Do you need me to stop at one of the restrooms in the park or...?"

"I think I can make it back to *Mom and Dad's*." She giggled.

"I can't wait to see Daddy again. I liked him. Skip skip skip..."

This time Vivika bit her tongue. But agreed with the little girl.

Chapter 16

Meanwhile, with the *kids* gone for their tour, Dad scrounged up several family photo albums and Billy's scrapbook, and stacked it on the end of two tables he slid together for a family dinner upon their return.

"Robert, you know that will just embarrass your son to death."

"Ahh, he'll get over it. What do you think of his Vivika?"

"I like her. She's quieter than I expected."

"She'll warm up. I know her type. Shy and reserved, then POW, she's one of us!" Dad was beside himself. Billy brought a girl home on the first date. It had never happened before, even with the one girl he dated for a year. He stopped and counted. Six months before he brought her home to meet *the* parents. This Vivika was someone very special.

"I hope you're right."

"Momma you always worry too much. She'll be fine, you'll see."

"They're here Robert, they're here. How's my hair?"

"Fine Momma, you look fine. Stop worrying."

Dad and Momma met them at the door and ushered them in like royalty. "Come, sit, sit." Dad invited them both in, more so Vivika than his son. He pulled her chair out for her. "What would you like to drink?" Dad asked.

"Some tea would be nice."

"Coming right up. Billy, get our guest an iced tea!" Dad instructed.

Billy shrugged his shoulders as he stood up from his chair. He caught Vivika's expression, "It's ok. I used to work here."

She smiled, "Be good or no tip."

"So tell me how you liked your tour?" Dad inquired.

Momma scooted a chair up to Vivika's left side and Dad sat in his chair to her right, both waiting on her review like it was news from home.

"It was beautiful. The lake is gorgeous. And he took me up to the ranger lookout spot, way up on top."

"That is a great place to lay and star gaze." Dad said.

"I saw my very first satellite fly over. Wow that was something to see."

"Wait for the meteor showers." Momma said.

"Billy said the same thing."

Momma excused herself to the kitchen. Dinner was ready.

Billy returned with a serving tray with four iced teas, and put one down at each place setting. Then he went back into the kitchen to help Momma bring dishes, bowls, and platters out to the table.

"This truly is special. I hope you didn't do this just for me?" Viv asked.

"Of course we did, and why shouldn't we?" Dad replied. "You're our guest and guests get special treatment."

"Tomorrow they'll make you a waitress!" Billy interjected.

"Hush." Momma scolded. "That takes at least two weeks and you know it." She said and they all laughed.

Dinner was a very pleasant and casual affair. The dinner chatter focused mainly on what the dishes were, where did Momma come up with the recipe for the mole' sauce, how long had they had the restaurant, and the dessert, with a few minutes spent solely on the hot springs and weather.

"It does get hot and some years we're lucky to get an inch of rain. Then other years the monsoons go on and on." Dad explained.

"It's a lot different than Seattle." Billy said.

"Almost everywhere I've traveled in the last year has been different than Seattle." Vivika said.

"Are you going to eventually return to Seattle?" Momma asked.

"Right now I'm not sure." She looked straight at Billy as she spoke. "I'm on some sort of journey, looking for where I belong." She tilted her head down.

"If you want my vote, I say you belong right here or at least within twenty miles of home, oops, I mean our home." Dad grinned as the intended blessing for her to stay nearby was delivered to both Vivika and Billy.

"Dad!" Billy protested.

Momma sensed something amiss. "Billy let's clear the table. C'mon, hurry up."

The scrumptious dinner had lasted nearly forty minutes, but the event was just getting started. The table was cleared and wiped down. Dad moved Vivika and himself to the end of the table. Huddled close, like two kids studying for a test or sharing gossip, Dad pulled the first photo album from the stack, laid it in front of Vivika and told her to open it.

"Oh look how young all of you are." She said. Vivika looked down at 30, 40 year-old pictures, and some much older from Dad and Momma's parents' collection of photos.

They thumbed through the first album, with Dad and Momma acting as the tour guides of the evolution of their lives and those of their children.

Vivika learned what each of the kids looked like from birth through high school. Hair styles, fashion changes, and economic status were obvious to her as she scanned each picture with enthusiasm. Not having any current memory of her own childhood, she soaked up the possibilities that could have been for her.

"This scrapbook is all Billy." Momma said with reverence in her voice. "He's my special boy. But don't let him know that." Momma patted Vivika on the knee, a loving, motherly pat.

Vivika opened the scrapbook. There was Billy staring back at her, wide-eyed, sitting atop a horse, his little boy fear and excitement plastered across his face. "Awwww, how cute."

Billy returned from the kitchen at the same time. "Oh Dad, you didn't!" He recognized the scrapbook right off.

"You never mind Billy. She's a guest, it's ok." Momma said, waving him to a chair next to the spectacle.

Vivika turned the pages cautiously, wondering what metamorphous Billy would turn in the next picture. A picture of him in the choir, maybe age 12. There he was all decked out in a baseball uniform. He was shooting a basketball in some high school game from a newspaper photo. The next few pages were football photos, team picture, Billy down in a three point stance, holding a football in the end zone. Under the plastic sleeves were game programs, score sheets, all of it becoming boring to Vivika. Report cards from first grade through his second year of college. She flipped another page and he was standing next to another guy, both with dark blue sweat shirts and matching sweat pants, New Mexico Highway Patrol Academy in white block letters on their chests.

"I'm so proud of him." Momma said and dabbed at a tear.

"This is when he first saw you." Dad said.

"Dad she wouldn't remember me. That

was so long ago." Billy said in her defense.

A flyer announcing an upcoming gymnastics meet in Albuquerque, dated six years prior. Her name was listed number two on a list of thirty names. Next to her name, a brief resume, two time National winner, Olympic alternate.

"That was when I was still at the academy. We were on a training day at the civic center. Crowd control, security, stuff like that. I was on the floor when you did your floor routine." Billy said.

On the next page, she was shocked to see someone who looked like her, in mid air, upside down, in some sort of twisted position.

"Did you take this picture?" Vivika asked.

"Just a lucky shot." He turned his head.

The next three pages were dedicated to her. Several newspaper clippings, more flyers, and ads with her name listed on them with some prominence. Another page had a People Magazine article about the U.S. gymnastics team hopefuls, with a short interview with her. Her hand trembled lightly as she read her own, yet unrecognizable words: "I've been training six hours a day with the team. I think we have a great chance of making the Olympics. And this time I won't be an alternate."

She looked at Billy. He didn't understand her expression. Terror. He knew who she was, but she didn't. And he had a scrapbook dedicated to her?

"Oh dear, here comes old Marv." Momma

stood up and went to the door to help the old man into the restaurant.

"Hey Marv!" Dad called out.

"How are you Robert? The food any good in this joint?" Marv smiled. He had been a regular since the day after they opened for business. Vivika welcomed the distraction of the old gentleman coming in, and just like the barber shop, it took him five minutes from the front door to sit down at a table. Momma stayed by his side the whole time, and took his order before she walked away.

Vivika was getting lightheaded, but her fingers could tell she was on the last page. She might as well be done with the mess and ask to be taken back to her hotel.

She turned the page and there was some sort of newspaper folded in half, just stuck in between the pages. Vivika opened the newspaper to find that it was the National Tab, dated two years ago. A messed up version of her lying in a hospital bed sent her reeling. Head spinning, she slipped from the chair before any of them could catch her.

"Go get me a cold wet towel. Now Billy!" Momma shouted.

"Vivika, are you ok?" Dad asked as he felt her forehead. She was cold and clammy.

Billy came back and stood over her. He handed the towel to Momma, his work pager and cell phone went off at the same time. He looked at the pager, "all officers respond." He flipped open his phone. "Montez. Yes sir, I can be there in about fifteen minutes." He flipped the phone closed. "I have to leave. There's an emergency out on I-25 and they want all units to respond. Sounds pretty bad. This could take all night. Dad, would you mind taking Vivika back to her hotel?"

"Not in this condition. We'll move her into the house until she feels better. You go, we'll take care of her. Go!"

"Hey kid, you don't look so hot."

"No shit?" She was coming to, but not all at once.

Momma and Dad looked at her as she spoke the "bad" word, then at each other. "Must be some kind of dream or something?" Momma said.

They helped Vivika pass through the kitchen, on the way to the portion of the restaurant that was their home. There were three bedrooms, two baths. The living room was plain, but comfortable, not overly loaded with junk or cluttered. Vivika was able to move on her own power, and made her way to the large sofa under a huge bay window, with a view of Elephant Butte promontory point. She was feeling better. Less spinning. The shock of seeing the post-op pictures was too much for her. On one hand she felt the old fight or flight building up. But deep inside, she couldn't remember ever feeling so safe and loved. Momma and Dad were pampering, scurrying around if she blinked.

Truth or Consequences

"What do you need sweetie?" Momma would ask. Dad brought a fresh pitcher of ice water and another cool wet towel for her forehead. Momma unfolded a blanket on the back of the couch and spread it over Vivika. Motherly loving hands tucked it around her. "Are you feeling better.", "Is there anything we can get you?" She assured them both that she was feeling better and soon she should go to her hotel room and get out of their way, that she didn't mean to be a bother.

"We won't hear of it, Vivika. There's plenty of room right here. We'll put some fresh sheets on one of the kids' old beds. You don't need to be moving around so much."

"No really, all my things are at the hotel. I'll just go straight to sleep. I'll be fine."

"Robert, go get all of her things and bring them back here. Our girl needs to be still and relax."

"No really, I don't want to put you two out." She rose up off of the couch to defend her decision, but a spasm of dizziness sent her right back down.

"See, sweetie, you're still not right. Robert, go get her things right now." Momma demanded.

"I'll be right back." Dad clamored around for his truck keys and wallet. He motioned for Momma to come near. "Which hotel is she at?"

"The Desert one at the north end of town. The one Barb runs."

"Oh, okay, I'll be back in a few minutes."

Vivika had her eyes closed with the cool towel over them. She couldn't quite make out what the two were talking about. But she guessed. "Here is my hotel key. You'll need it." The slight movement brought a wave of nausea. She clamped her eyes tighter. She just knew she would spin off of the couch at any second.

Dad snatched the key from her hand as he walked across the room and out the side door of the residence.

"Spinning, spinning, we're spinning, yay."

"I don't need you reminding me." Vivika said.

"Poor dear." Momma sat holding Vivika's hand.

Chapter 17

Officer Montez was called into a mess. Every emergency vehicle in the county greeted him when he arrived on scene. Highway patrol, city police, county sheriff's deputies, ambulances, fire and rescue. He parked on the shoulder thirty or so yards from the epicenter of the activity, retrieved his service weapon and a dark blue windbreaker with reflective letters that read HIGHWAY PATROL across the back. The last time he saw this much activity was when they did a full on mutual response disaster drill.

"What the hell is going on?" Montez asked his supervisor.

"We have a shooting. The sniper." A helicopter swooped over head with his one million candle power spotlight splaying over the scene below. "Hang on." He told Montez. "Alpha One, follow the arroyo up."

Montez looked around. There was a car on the roadway, partially covered with a yellow plastic tarp. It was a discreet way to cover a body. The bright yellow gave it away, but the onlookers couldn't see the gore, be it a traffic accident or, in this case, a shooting victim.

"Montez." His supervisor's voice brought him back from the yellow tarp.

"Yes, sir?"

"Get up there and use some of that special training in tracking you have?"

"Yes, sir."

"I want you to head up that arroyo or around the back if there's a way. Get up there and have a look around. It looks like the shot came from that direction. We have a team up there now looking for evidence, but I want you to look for tracks and get back to me. Go."

"I'm on it." Montez knew the arroyo like he knew the rangers' lookout. He jogged over to a highway patrol SUV unit, told the officer he needed it, orders from the supervisor. He jumped in the SUV and drove through the morass of vehicles and flashing lights. It didn't take him long to find the cut-off he wanted. He turned off the highway, down the embankment, turned right and headed back toward the lights. Then he took a hard right into the arroyo, using the underpass. He pulled out of the arroyo, and up onto a 4x4 trail running parallel to the arroyo. After ten bumpy minutes, he was near the top of the hill. He could see flashlights zipping around ahead of him. The other team was searching for empty shell casings, cigarette butts, beer cans, any kind of evidence they could use.

Montez got out of the SUV with flashlight in hand. He could track, humans, and animals, and was adept at following signs most people never considered.

He started examining the ground as soon as he turned on the flashlight. Any disturbance in the soil, or a twig on a bush out of place, could mean something to his trained eye. He moved in a sweeping pattern until he reached the others at the site they were scouring.

"Anything?" Montez asked Jenkins, the lead on this end of the investigation.

"Nothing yet. Something was going on up here, but I can't tell exactly what yet." Jenkins said.

"So we're guessing someone was perched up here and shot down toward the highway?"

"The trajectory on the victim tells us that much. A witness reported a muzzle flash up in this area."

"Got it. I'll be on the other side of your team, moving up and over the hill. Holler if you find something." Montez said.

"Good luck up there." Jenkins replied.

Montez had been up on the hill one time, ten years prior. It still looked the same even at night. This location was hike-in only. No access by road. Someone would have to park at the base of the other side of the hill and hoof it up there. He vaguely remembered it was about a quarter mile to the base of the hill. Long damn hike with a rifle, just to get off one round and go back down the hill.

He proceeded with his flashlight sweep. He quickly ruled out several sets of footprints as those of the other search team, then he stopped, looked back at the scene where Jenkins was moving around, then looked ahead again. How would I come over the hill, go down there, set up, shoot, and then come back up? Montez shined his powerful flashlight up at the top of the hill, moving it slowly along the tops of the mesquite bushes, back and forth. Finally, he spotted what he was looking for. An almost imperceptible V in the outline of the bushes. The V was caused by someone pushing through the bushes. He froze, dead still. Now, before he took another step, he needed to follow the trail down from the V. He found it and stepped wide off to the side to avoid contaminating the suspect's trail.

Finding the V was key. Still damn near impossible, but he exploited the night by using the spotlight beam of his flashlight to focus only on the V, and the trail, coming and going. In the daylight, with the entire area bathed in sunlight, he would be distracted by anything that moved or looked suspicious.

Montez made it up to the V, and then took the painstaking journey to the end of the trail. Over his right shoulder, to the east, the dark night sky was being edged out by the sunrise. The trail ended at the bottom of the hill, and melded into a seldom used road.

"Bravo one zero."

"Go ahead Montez." His supervisor responded.

"Whoever did the shooting covered their tracks."

"Say again?"

"The shooter swept the road with some mesquite. No tire tracks. And no tracks on the hill. Only a couple of broken branches."

"A-firm. Same as the last couple of times?" His supervisor held his breath for a heartbeat.

"Yes."

"Dammit. Have the crew up there get pictures, and anything else you find, and then wrap it up."

"Copy that."

Montez was bone tired. The day before had been full, a date with Vivika, dinner, then out on the hillside all night. But he had another two hours of hands on work, then paperwork, a full briefing, and eventually catch up to Vivika.

* * * * *

The sniper slept in the next morning. No rushing around for him. No overtime or paperwork. He planned on going fishing and maybe take a dip at his favorite hot springs. Too soon for another side hill trek with his rifle. Besides his arm was sore from last night. He looked at the clock. Too early. He rolled over, tucked his pillow under his neck tight, and went back to sleep, leaving the clean-up for the professionals.

* * * * *

Montez stopped at his place for a shower and a change of clothes before stopping by Vivika's hotel room. He knocked and waited. He knocked again. Nothing. Turning on his heel, he double checked that her car was still in the parking space. He pulled his cell phone and called his Mother.

"Hi son."

"Where is Vivika?" Concerned with a pissy attitude from no sleep.

"She's here with your father and me."

Relieved, but still pissy. "Why?"

"We thought it best that she stay put. Your father went to her hotel and brought all belongings back here. She doesn't need to be alone right now."

He couldn't argue with that logic, but still. "Ok, I'll be right over."

Montez beat himself up for leaving her there and for ever having kept that damn National Tab in his scrapbook, but what were the chances of her parking on the shoulder of I-25 on his patrol? He only saved the flyer from that day because it was part of his law enforcement training. A gold star day and he wanted to save it. And why in the hell would his Dad show that to her? Dammit! He slugged the steering wheel. She probably thinks he's a stalker. Damn damn damn!

Ten minutes later he pulled up in front of the family restaurant. Vivika was standing at the front door. He sheepishly walked up to her.

"That was some first date Officer Montez!" She said with a smile. "No good night kiss or nothing."

He was speechless. "I, I…"

Truth or Consequences

"You haven't asked me yet, but I'm not sure about a second date. No way to treat a lady. Abandoning me with these horrible people!" She laughed.

"I'm so, so sorry." His head downcast.

"Yep, horrible people. Held my hand through the night. Cold towels, comfortable bed, great food, great company, horrible way to treat a first date."

"How can I make it up to you? I can't believe you saw that scrapbook, how I kept that stuff," She cut him off.

"Your Dad explained the whole thing." Vivika stood with a hand on her hip, looking at him, his head down, no doubt embarrassed. She walked up to him. "Hey you." He didn't look up. She touched his chin and raised his head. "It's ok." She gently pressed her lips to his. "Honest, everything is fine. How about if you ask me out for a second date?"

"Seconds and thirds dahling."

"Vivika, would you like to go out on a second date?"

"With a flake like you?" They both burst into laughter, and she hugged him. Momma and Dad watched from the front windows inside the restaurant.

*   *   *   *   *

The sniper finished his hot springs dunk and headed for Elephant Butte Lake to try and kill some fish. He drove his truck with his boat in tow, right down Main Street. Four people on the sidewalk waved to him as he passed by. He was one of *them*.

Chapter 18

Portia only had one choice: follow Coach Perv to where Vivika was. The chances of breaking into his place one more time and not getting caught weren't good. Henderson was a dead end. Stromberg has the info he needed to find her, so there was no way Portia could warn Vivika in time, even if she hand delivered another letter to Henderson. What were the odds of Vivika getting a warning letter in time? She had to act.

"Hi Tim, this is Portia." She called her boss at the rehab facility.

"Hey Portia, what's up?" Typical boss attitude dripping through the phone.

"I need a leave of absence."

"A what?"

"I need a leave of absence for a month."

"Impossible. You've only been here, what, six or seven months. No way."

"Then consider this my resignation. I quit."

"Now wait just a damn minute. You can't leave me hanging like this."

"Mail me my last check. When I get back in town I'll swing by and clean out my locker." Portia was smiling, why, she didn't know. Yet.

"Don't bother, I'll box it all up with your check." He hung up on her.

She kept smiling as she packed a bag, "A

week, two?" She looked at her suitcases, deciding whether to pack two or three. "Could be three weeks or a month." She packed all three, basically cleaning out her dresser and more than half the contents of the closet.

"Hopefully the perv hasn't woken up yet." She was coaching herself as she approached his house. She blew out a sigh of relief. She was counting on his vodka usage, and him sleeping off his drunk from the night before. It was just before noon, and she had been waiting for two hours, when he came out of his house, threw a large gym bag in the trunk of his car, and drove off with her on his tail. No plan, just follow him. Try not to lose his trail. With no idea of where he was headed, she'd have to stay on her toes. At least her hybrid would out-perform his big assed truck, and with her 36 mpg, he would have to stop three times as often.

Not having a mortgage or needing to pay rent for almost two years had really helped out Portia's savings account. She made some rough calculations and she could be out of work for about five months. So, however far the Coach traveled on his quest for Vivika, she would be right there with him.

Portia expected Coach Perv to drive like a wild truck driver on meth. The opposite was true. He drove at 4 mph under the speed limit. Probably from years of his dedicated drunk driving.

She liked that he was traveling south. She

hadn't been out of Seattle in years. Other than following him, she would do her best to enjoy the ride, the grand adventure of it all.

On her way to his house that morning, she made a quick stop into a beauty supply store and purchased five wildly differing wigs. Blonde, long and short, black, straight, short and long.

Her confidence was high. She gripped the steering wheel tighter, made a face, and played with the words running through her mind: the hunter and the hunted. A series of quotes from movies and TV interrupted the word play. "I'm gonna get you sucka." She smiled. "I'm on a mission from God." Another smile appeared as she replayed one of her favorites from her childhood, "I'm a chicken hawk and you're a chicken!" She cracked herself up. Portia touched the "shuffle" button on her CD changer and pressed herself into the driver's seat, "I'm a chicken hawk and you're a chicken."

Portia never spotted the car that followed her.

* * * * *

He had his travel mug filled with vodka next to him in the center console, and plenty more where that came from. Coach Stromberg was oblivious to the two vehicles that followed him.

The little bitch was in New Mexico of all places. Fifteen hundred miles from Seattle. His

GPS device showed it would take 24 hours of driving. Stopping for food and gas, he thought maybe two days of hard driving. Four quarts of vodka might be enough to get him there.

His plan was simple. Find her and bring his wife home. Have her put him on her new accounts, get his cash flow back up and flowing, divorce her. Or maybe she'd have another accident and not survive next time. The poor little bitch.

He made her what she was, and she loses her leg and runs away like he didn't matter? Not!! She owed him for all his hard work. She blew it, not him, and she thinks she can just run off and live the good life and leave him in the dust? She owed him, and she would pay up, or else.

Chapter 19

"Well, since all of my stuff is here, why don't you give me a ride back to the hotel so I can pick up my car and pay my bill?" Vivika asked Billy.

"You're not going to stay with these crazy people?" A mystified Billy replied.

"Why not? I would insult them by not staying. I can't tell you the last time I felt this comfortable and safe. Your mom and dad are great."

"Try living with them for twenty years!" He looked down and kicked at the gravel. "Ok, if this is what you want."

"Besides, I'll be able to see you more often, right?" She asked through a sly grin.

"More than likely. I do come by here a lot."

"It's settled then. My car and lunch. Then you can tell me all about your exciting night."

They stepped into the restaurant to let the parental units know they were leaving for a little while. "Will you be back for dinner?" Momma asked a hopeful tone in her voice.

"Yes." Vivika answered before Billy could react or make up an excuse.

Vivika and Billy left for her car. "What was so important that you had to leave last night?" She asked.

"There was a problem out on I-25."

"Must have been pretty important to call you in, while you were off duty."

"A shooting."

"On the highway?"

"Yes. And it's not the first time. It's a sniper. He shows up every five or six months. Nothing consistent, other than the ammunition he uses and his accuracy."

"Sounds pretty serious. No wonder you were called out."

Pregnant silence fell between them as he drove to the hotel.

"And you didn't get any sleep, did you?" Vivika asked.

"No. I finished up, took a shower, threw on some fresh clothes, and came right over to see how you were. You didn't answer the door at the hotel, so I called my mom to find out about you. Man, what a surprise."

"That scrapbook of yours threw me for a loop. I never saw that tabloid thing before last night."

"You're kidding?"

"No, not at all. The date on the cover is a week after I left Seattle. I never saw it."

"Were the pictures doctored, or was that how you looked after the accident and surgery?"

"Apparently that's what I looked like. I was pretty beat up."

"It's not a stretch those came out of some personal medical file?"

"Apparently. Pull into that burger place, I

want a soda."

"Kicking the Slurpee habit?" He laughed.

"No, I just don't know where one is."

"You know, I'm sort of a cop. I know all the convenience stores. We can get you a Slurpee."

"Cool, let's go."

Montez zig zagged through the hills and popped out on the main street, heading south. Near the end of town, he pulled into a Circle Stop convenience store. They both got out and went inside.

"Hey Billy." A store-bought blonde greeted him from behind the counter, and then sneered as Vivika caught up to him.

"Hi Steph." He went straight to the Slurpee machine. "Here ya go. Red or blue frozen sugar water?" He chuckled.

"I'm in the mood for red today. And some Corn Nuts."

They bought the junk food, ignoring the attitude from Steph, then left the store. Around the corner from the front door was a battered and barely usable picnic table. She suggested they sit down for a while.

"Montez."

"Please Miss Stryker call me Billy."

"And it's Viv to you, ok?"

"Glad that's settled."

"Me too. Based on the scrapbook, you knew who I was when you talked to me the other day." She got right to the point.

"Actually, I knew the instant I read your name on your license."

"Are you my stalker or number one fan?" She asked.

"Like I told you. It was a training session from the academy. I just thought it would be cool to keep a couple of souvenirs. Nothing more. And finding you on the highway the other day..."

"You what? Felt sorry for me?"

"Not at all. I have some discretion when it comes to giving a written or verbal warning or arresting someone. You looked like you needed some rest."

"Easy kid, next you'll ask him to jump in the hot springs with you." She could hear the echo of Grumpy's giggle.

"Like that would be a bad thing." She talked back to Grumpy.

"Exactly." Billy said.

"Exactly what?" She asked.

"Nothing." He noticed a pattern with her odd comments.

"Do you have a favorite hot springs in town?" She went to the heart of it again.

"I have a couple that I use. Why?"

"You were up all night. Maybe I could treat you to a soak?"

"Hmm..."

"Don't worry, we don't have to tell your mom and dad. They don't expect us back until dinner anyway."

"Sounds really great right now." He

smiled.

Montez drove away from the little store and was soon passing Bill and Edith's Hot Springs. One block past their place, he pulled into one of the first fully paved parking lots Viv had seen in town. This hot springs screamed class. A large landscaped area in front of the building, replete with a waterfall and cacti of all sizes and colors. Freshly painted wrought iron fencing about the perimeter of the property. The main building looked brand new, with no chipped paint around the windows, the front door painted a bright Chinese red, and the signage fresh and bold, welcoming her to Casa de Agua Fuego.

"Wow, this is nice." Vivika said.

"It's one of my favorites."

She stood waiting for him to grab something out of the trunk of the car. "I always carry a change of clothes."

"Lucky me. Where's mine?"

"Shit." He was caught flat footed.

"It's fine Billy. Don't worry." She said.

"It's not that."

"What then?"

"You'll see."

They entered the establishment and stepped to the counter. Viv couldn't take her eyes off of the décor. A mix of Plains Indian art, Navajo, and Mexican interior design work.

"Billy! How are you? I heard about last night. And who is this?" The statuesque woman behind the counter was definitely no Edith, no desert rat as they refer to themselves around here. Long blonde hair, with a few streaks of pure white mixed in. It nearly matched her white cotton peasant blouse. The stark white blouse accentuated her cleavage, and the perfectly colored Squash Blossom necklace set the whole look off.

"This is-"

"I'm Vivika Stryker." Viv reached across the counter and shook the woman's hand.

"Nice to meet you Vivika. I'm Claudia Banker, owner."

"I'm just a tourist and friend of the local sheriff." She feigned a lilting southern accent.

"Oookay, and I guess you two want a dip in the hot springs?"

"Yes please." Billy was terrified. Vivika picked up on his apprehension.

"Looks like you'll need towels." Claudia's voice belied her nervousness.

"Just towels, thanks." Viv fired another round.

"Here you go. I gave you room nine. It has the most *privacy*." Her voice dripping with jealousy.

"Thanks Claudia." Billy took the towels and key, and walked toward the room with his head down.

Once inside the room, Viv asked, "What's with the hanging head?"

"Everyone in town will know you were here with me."

"So?"

"It's a small town Viv. The rumors, shit."

"There'll be rumors about both of us then. Don't sweat it. Get it? Hot springs, don't sweat it?" She smiled, not taking too much pleasure in his discomfort. "Not to mention, Claudia didn't see us bring any suits in with us!" She laughed and slugged him in the arm.

"Oh god." He was mortified.

"C'mon before the water cools off." She slipped off her shoes, pushed down her sweat pants, took off her sweat top, and leaving her panties on, stepped into the tub. Her arms crossed across her bare chest. She turned the valve to usher in the hot mineral water, put the drain pipe in place. "C'mon on in!" She shouted over the sound of the rushing water.

He was standing near the door with his back turned to her. "I'll wait until the tub is full, that way you can cover up with the water."

"Whatever you want Billy." The high volume pressure already had the water at her knees. "Won't be long now."

"Fine." He stood patiently.

Billy's fears were founded. Before the tub was full of hot mineral water, Claudia was on the phone. She called two people, and they called two people, and so on. By the time he and Viv were out of the tub and dried off, his parents would hear it 14th hand, though they didn't mind at all that their lonesome son might have found someone. He needed someone and she was a good girl.

"I didn't bring you here with an agenda. Just a platonic soak in the hot springs." He said.

"Whatever you want Billy. The tub is full and I'm in the far corner, so come on in." She was in fact in the far corner, neck deep in the water.

He turned quick to make sure she was where she said she was. He eased up to the tub, leaving his boxers on, and stepped down into the water.

"I can see why you like coming here. It's very, hmm spa like, compared to Bill and Edith's."

"Claudia has really done a lot of remodeling and updating. This place used to look almost as bad as Bill and Edith's."

"Wow, she really has done a good job."

He sat on the steps, the hot water up to his neck. The reflection of the shimmering water prevented him from an accidental peek at her. They soaked in silence. They glimpsed one another looking toward each other.

Instead of a simple timer to let customers know their time was up, Claudia personally went to each room and knocked. A tinge of jealousy forced her hand to be heavier than usual and pounded the door. "BILLY, TIME'S UP!"

The loudness startled them both. "Thanks!" Billy answered her. He looked at Viv, "Guess our soak is over?"

"Ya think? She is hot for you Billy."

"Claudia? No way."

"Oh well, I'm done with my soak." She moved toward the steps to get out, keeping an arm across her chest.

Billy was confused. Did he wait for her or get out and drip dry? He didn't wait long for the answer. As Viv neared the steps, she dropped her arm and put her hand on his shoulder, "Ladies first," and walked up the steps leaving him in the water. He stayed there waiting for her to towel off and dress.

"Coast is clear. You can come out now." She stood holding a towel for him.

An instant pang of worry hit him as he looked at her playful grin. He moved up a step, she moved back a step.

"C'mon Viv." He half heartedly pleaded.

"What? Here's your towel, Officer Montez." Her grin widened to a smile.

Another step for him, and one for her.

Billy's waterlogged boxers slipped down his hips as he made his way out of the tub.

"Officer Montez, I hope that weapon is waterproof?" He laughed.

His right hand dropped to his side, groping for the elastic waist band, his left hand reaching out for the towel, sloshing water and slipping as he bolted for it.

Viv turned her head, blushing and laughing, and handed him the towel.

"You're not nice!" He growled, and then broke into a belly laugh.

Giggling and teasing one another, he dressed and they walked out of the tub room. Once in the hallway, the duo noticed that Claudia was only a few steps ahead of them, heading back to the check in counter. Viv and Billy looked at each other, "Now the whole town knows you're a slut." She said to him. They both laughed so hard that Claudia turned and looked at them.

Not a word was spoken as they signed out on the register and paid the bill. Claudia was incensed, and would not make eye contact with the couple. They both held their stomachs while they laughed their way outside to his car.

They were still laughing as he drove away and his cell phone rang, "Hello."

"Hi Billy."

"Hi Mom." He was trying to contain his laughter, but Viv was letting hers out full blast.

"Sounds like you two are having a great time." Momma said.

"Yes. Just the destruction of my reputation."

"I see. Could you do your dear sweet mother a small favor?"

He took a deep breath to calm his giggle. "Name it."

"For some reason we are out of sour cream here at the restaurant. Could you swing by the store and pick up three quarts for me?"

"Absolutely. Anything else?"

"I think that's all. If there's anything else I'll call you."

"Ok Mom." He was gazing at Viv, half listening to his mother.

"I guess Claudia should change the name of the business to Laughing Waters. Bye Billy." She ended the call before he could respond.

"Oh shit." He couldn't help but laugh.

"What?" Viv asked.

"My mother already knows we were at Claudia's!"

Mockingly, she half shouted, "Your own mother knows you're a slut!" They howled with laughter.

A few blocks later, he pulled in the parking lot of the grocery store. He explained what his mother had called for. They left the car and headed into the store. Crossing the parking lot, Viv reached out and took his hand in hers.

"Good job kid." Grumpy complimented her.

"Thanks." She said automatically.

"Dahling he looks scrumptious wet."

"I know huh." Another response.

"You're welcome." Billy said, without knowing the real reason behind her comments.

Still giggly, they walked up and down each isle of the store tossing odd items into the shopping cart: wooden matches, balsamic vinegar, two jars of baby food (strained peas), one quart of 30 weight motor oil, a 24 count package of diapers, and a one gallon jar of pickled eggs, but not forgetting the three quarts of sour cream. They hoped the odd items would be a funny joke to play on his mother.

The laughter ended after they went through the check out and pushed the basket closer to his car. All four tires on Billy's car were flat. Long gashes in the sidewalls of the tires left no doubt that it was a warning. On the back windshield in the fine silt of desert dust someone had written with a fingertip, "Leave me alone!"

"What the..." In total shock, Billy walked around his car, looking at the complete assassination of his tires.

Viv stood back, the laughter buzz evaporated with the air in the tires.

"The old man is snoring." Viv heard the end of the rhyme as the child's voice faded.

Chapter 20

The three vehicles traveling southbound on Interstate 5 fell through Washington, Oregon, and into and out of central California without bumping into each other at fuel, food or rest stops.

Coach Stromberg, although drunk, was able to drive his drive four miles per hour under the speed limit, undetected by the sparse law enforcement.

Portia dealt with each stop-and-go with white knuckled acuteness. Stopping at opposite fuel islands at gas stations, changing wigs on the fly to go inside the mini-marts and grab snacks, and high energy drinks, then zipping back to her car before the Coach had time to spot her.

The followers, stayed fresh and on their toes. This was no game to them. Trained in pursuits, tailing, and covert surveillance, this was nothing but another day at work for them. Their vehicle was equipped with an extra gas tank. The vehicle's non-stop range was over 600 miles. A 72-quart ice chest provided them with all the food and drinks they needed for four days on the road. Following a subject was no joke for them, and they were ready for all contingencies.

Chapter 21

"Somebody doesn't like you." Viv said. Her heart sank.

"I get that part." Billy said.

"Like you said, it's a small town. Maybe you pissed somebody off when you pulled them over and gave them a ticket?" She suggested, hoping there would be a simple explanation and a non-violent ending.

"I'll call my Dad to come pick you up."

"I can wait with you." Viv said.

Billy noticed something on the hood of the car, right in front of the driver's view. A small sprig of mesquite. He moved closer and examined it. Within a half inch of the dark green-tipped sprig was a circle, with two opposing lines drawn through it by a fingertip. It was a caricature of a rifle scope crosshairs. The hair on his neck stood up. Instinctively he reached for his weapon, usually in its holster on his right hip. It was still in the trunk of the car. His head turned to survey his surroundings. Mostly buildings, houses and businesses, no high points, no hilly hideout for the sniper. Nonetheless, he needed, wanted, some cover for Viv and himself.

"Let's go back in the store so I can make some calls."

"Ok." Viv agreed, unaware the depth of the threat.

Billy took her by the elbow, eyes

constantly scanning the area. He wondered if he'd hear the report of the rifle, or would the bullet just slam into him?

Once inside the store, he maneuvered them away from windows and did his best to put a concrete wall between them and the outside world. Viv did not notice that he was standing guard, running interference between her and everything else. He positioned her at the magazine rack, with his back to her. She looked over the titles of the skimpy rack. Meanwhile, he called his supervisor and spilled the details of the evidence on his car. The supervisor instructed Montez to stay inside, away from the windows, and he would personally respond with an all unit alert. Then Montez called his Dad.

"Dad."

"What's wrong Billy?" He could hear the difference in his son's voice. Official and fearful.

"I need you to come up to the grocery store and pick Vivika up and take her back to the restaurant. But I need you to wait across the street in the parts house's parking lot until it's safe."

"I'm on my way. What's this all about?"

"The sniper is getting personal. Slashed my tires and left a warning on the hood of my car."

"Okay Billy, I'll be there and wait for your call."

"Thanks Dad."

Viv thumbed through pages and pages of a glossy magazine, glancing at models and interviews with celebrities she didn't recognize.

Montez paced to the edge of the huge store windows, sneaking a peek, to see if the cavalry had shown up yet, and then back to Viv's side. He looked down the well-lit-aisles of the store, the people standing in the checkout line, vehicles moving outside, then back at Viv. She was barely a new friend, but he was prepared to protect her from anyone.

He heard the sirens, roaring engines, and screeching tires. Another look out the window. His safety net arrived just short of guns a "blazing". For a split second he visualized it was 1895, dust and dirt flying, fifteen men on horseback galloping into town to rescue the local sheriff from deadly bandits.

"Stay put for a few minutes." He told Viv.

"Sure." She was deep into an article on "24 ways to turn your mate on."

"Oh dahling, number 18 is wonderful."

"I know, I can't wait to try it out."

Officer Montez exited the store and went straight to his supervisor's car.

"Where are you parked?" On the job and deadly serious.

"Right over there." Montez pointed his disabled vehicle then took off toward it, his supervisor following behind.

Within minutes, yellow crime scene tape was strung from parking lot light poles to patrol cars that were parked in a circle around Montez's vehicle. Circle the wagons, fitting, Montez started to grin.

"And this is how you found it?" His supervisor asked. "Nothing was touched?"

"Of course not." He replied slightly offended.

"Just checking."

The supervisor barked orders, and men and women moved with deliberate motion. Pictures were taken. One technician videotaped the car, the parking lot, and the store.

"I want the exits to the parking lot closed and everyone in the store interviewed. Get the license plates of every damn car, truck, and Moped in this parking lot. Maybe we'll get lucky."

Officers were stationed at the entrance to the store. The parking lot exits were blocked with patrol cars, funneling all outbound traffic to one exit. One officer stood guard at the rear of the store. It was a total lock down. And thirty minutes too late. Billy and Viv had horsed around in the store for at least that long.

The supervisor guessed it was too late. The interview answers were all the same. I didn't see anyone or anything out of the ordinary. No, I didn't hear anything. Nothing out of the ordinary.

Montez called his Dad, anxiously waiting across the street. "It's all clear. Come on over and pick Viv up now."

The supervisor gave the OK for Montez to access the trunk of his car to retrieve his sidearm and badge. Billy no longer felt naked. Weapon in place, he was at least able to return fire if the sniper showed his hand.

Robert Montez pulled his 4 x 4 truck right up to the yellow crime scene tape. All the officers on scene knew him and waved him through the morass of uniforms and vehicles. He looked to his son. Billy held up his hand to signal he was to wait for him to bring Vivika out.

Billy jogged back to the store where Vivika was still reading her magazine. "Viv, Dad's here to take you home."

"Home?"

"Back to the restaurant."

"I can wait with you."

"No, this is going to take a while. No need for you to stand around and be bored out of your head."

"Ok if you think that's best?"

"And Momma is waiting for the sour cream. C'mon, I'll walk you out."

She noticed the concern on his face and how he escorted her out of the store. He walked her straight to his father's waiting truck, opened the door, and helped her in. "Ok Dad, take care of her. I'll be home after we get finished up here."

"You gonna be ok?" His Dad asked.

Billy Montez answered in a lightning fast sentence, in a language Vivika didn't understand. "The sniper left me a personal message on my car, slashed the tires, and he might still be hanging around out there somewhere."

"Ok Billy we'll see you when you come

home." In a fluid motion, he pulled away from the yellow tape and drove out of the parking lot.

Viv blew Billy a kiss as they drove away.

*   *   *   *   *

"Are you ok?" Robert asked Viv.

"I'm fine, why?"

"You've had a busy day is all." He didn't know how much she actually knew about what had happened to Billy's car.

"I had a great day. The hot springs was outstanding, again. I'm giving some serious thought of extending my stay."

"We would love for you stay longer!" Robert was grinning ear to ear.

"How is the housing market around here?"

"Same as the rest of the country right now. Pockets of good areas, pockets of real bad areas."

"Which areas do you like the best?" Viv, honestly curious.

"Let's drop that bag of groceries off and I'll take you to a couple of neighborhoods I like."

"Thanks Robert."

"Please, call me Dad."

"Ok, Dad, let's go looking at some houses." She looked out her window. She had a feeling, a sensation that prior to her accident she may or may not have ever felt. She thought this feeling was like coming home.

They dropped off the sour cream and bag of oddities to Momma and told her they were going out for a drive. Momma was all for it. She added her two cents about where to go to look at houses.

Robert drove up into the hills, through downtown Elephant Butte, then ventured further south, through Las Palomas canyon, Caballo, Hillsboro, and many places in a forty mile radius that only a locally grown boy would know of. Nothing hit Viv as a must see, or a second visit to settle her feelings. A house, even the most elaborate adobe or southwestern styling, did nothing for her. He drove, she looked, to no avail. He would ask her at every place he pointed out if she liked this house or this house? Nope, it just wasn't 'speaking' to her.

"What are you looking for?" Robert asked as he pulled onto a wide shoulder of the road and stopped.

"I just decided today that I might be interested in moving here. I have no clear idea of what kind of house or location I want yet." She replied.

"Well, I suggest that you don't settle on anything that isn't just right. You have a place to stay as long as you want. We can figure out the housing later." He smiled his best fatherly smile.

"How much would buying one of those hot springs spas cost?" Viv spoke without any internal editing. Something deep within nudged her, indicating this wasn't normal for her.

"Some you can pick up cheap, some are so run down that the city wants them bulldozed. Others, like Claudia's," he winked at her, "would probably cost a half mill easy. Is that what you're thinking of?"

"The idea is growing on me."

"You want to go into business?"

"It's a possibility, a long range kind of thing." She was brainstorming on the fly.

"Hey kid, go talk to Edith about her retirement plans."

"Can we stop at Bill and Edith's hot springs?"

"Sure can. It's only a few minutes from here. Can I ask a stupid question?"

"Sure."

"Did you leave something of value there? Not many reasons to go twice in a week to that dump."

"Call it a hunch, Dad." She smiled.

Robert giggled at hearing her call him Dad. He could get used to it real quick. "Fair enough."

As promised, they arrived at Bill and Edith's in no time. Edith raised her head up from a second hand paperback romance she was reading. Vivika registered in her mind, but Robert?

"Robert Montez is that you?" She exclaimed.

"Hi Edith, how are you, you ol' desert rat!"

"I'll be damned. Come here and give me a hug!"

Robert looked at Viv with a 'gee thanks a million' look.

"How are you?" Edith asked her old friend.

"Doing good. We never see you at the restaurant?"

"It's too far to drive and Bill doesn't drive after dark."

"How is Bill?" He asked. Viv stood to the side of the conversation, taking a good hard look at the exterior of the business. Lots of work, followed by lots of money. But doable if Edith was pliant.

"He's fine when he takes all of his meds. Hates going to the doctor, but he needs to see them almost once a month now, after his surgery."

"Nothing too serious, I hope?"

"Nah, just normal old people shit. Colon, prostate, diabetes, high blood pressure. The normal stuff. So what brings you out my way?"

"My house guest..."

"Hi ya kid. Vivika, right?"

"You remembered, yes, Vivika."

"What can I do ya for?" Too much stress, nicotine, and caffeine showed in her smile.

"With Bill's health problems, have you given any thought to retirement?"

"How's that?" Edith was caught off guard.

"Retiring, moving closer to the doctors."

"And how would we go about doing that?" The slip of a girl standing in front of her, almost being fresh, what could she do about it?

"Sell this place and go."

"Who said anything about selling?"

Robert stood in silence, studying Vivika. He knew Edith well enough and thought he knew how she would react, but this spitfire kid standing there, toe to toe, was holding her own.

"It's the logical thing to do, isn't it?" Vivika was getting nowhere.

"Robert, who is this, this, little girl to you?" Edith asked.

"She's a house guest. She feels like a daughter." Robert looked Edith in the eye, as if to say, you might be pissed off, but keep it clean.

"Oh. And I suppose you want to buy this dump? With the leaky roof, bad wiring and..."

"Why not? Tell you what Edith, you think about it, give me a call at," She looked at Robert, "Momma and Dad's. You have the number."

"Umm." Mind running wild, Edith stood mouth agape and rubbing her right temple. "But."

"Think about it, and then make me an offer. I'm ready for dinner Dad." Vivika turned and walked back to the truck.

"But." Stunned. "Make *YOU* and offer?"

"Call me." Vivika said as she closed the door to the truck.

"Robert?" Edith was looking for any answer.

"I guess you need to think it over and call her. See ya Edith." Robert joined Vivika in the truck and they drove off.

"Did that accident you were in cause some sort of dain bramage?" He laughed at his play on words.

"I think so. I met Billy on the highway a couple of days ago, I'm living with you and Momma, and now I'm thinking of buying and remodeling Bill and Edith's nightmare. Yeah, I'm nuts I guess." She smiled at the thought of buying the rundown hot springs and breathing life into it. Maybe add a small bistro for the slow days. The smile felt good and the conversation with Edith felt right.

"Ok... since you put it that way, I guess it makes sense." Robert said, still shocked.

"Dad, I have one friend in Seattle, plus an attorney, that's it. I still have amnesia. Maybe I'm blocking some dark stuff and don't want to remember anything before the accident. I have an income, some savings, and I love it here."

Robert, a lifelong student of the road, and people, knew what Vivika was talking about. Why not stop? Why not try something new and different? He had. Chasing a bottle and wild women across five states only brought him home. It wasn't until he tried something different that he found he was in love with only one woman. The bottle was an empty friend that took him away to nothingness. "Why not, Vivika? I'll help any way I can." He stuck his hand out to shake on the promise. Her hand, the size of a child's, was swallowed up in his.

"Ok Dad, it's a deal."

"We have a daddy, skip, skip, skip..."

"Yes we do."

"Pardon?" Robert asked.

"Yes we do have a deal." Smiling. "Sometimes you just have to change directions, try something different."

"Viv, I think we're going to get along just fine."

Chapter 22

The sniper stepped up his next planned attack by one month. He had fired at seven vehicles in as many months, three dead, four wounded. The cops never figured out that they were not random attacks. He wanted four locals dead, period. What better way to off four people and not have them all connected. The ones he wounded, he did so by design. They would heal.

A profiler was brought in and the results were released to the press, a move of desperation on the cops' part. The profile, which he kept the newspaper clipping of, said the sniper probably had military training in order to make the shots that he had. Also, he was a white male between the ages of 29 and 45, single, skilled laborer, and in very good health, based on the terrain in proximity to the gunshots. One of the county deputies said the shooter had to be part mountain goat to get up and down some of the locations they found. Wrong, wrong, wrong!

Deputy Montez was getting too damn close. Number four was due for his date with the truth. He'd have to throw in Deputy Montez for free. The shooter struggled with one question: only wound him or take him all the way out?

* * * * *

Portia was wide awake and ready to go,

Truth or Consequences

but the perv hadn't moved. She even took the chance of walking past his car on the way to the restroom at the Westley rest stop on I-5. He was snoring! Of all the nerve, didn't he know he was wasting her time sitting still? Another trip to the restroom, and he was still snoring. A parking space opened up next to him. She backed out of her spot and pulled up next to him. She parked in his blind spot and waited.

The followers held their position and watched.

Portia waited another hour, and another round trip to the restroom, read the "You Are Here" sign, got a sip of water from a suspect drinking fountain, and headed back to the car. She had had enough. She put her seat all the way back and set off her factory car alarm. HONK HONK HONK HONK! With her window down, she could hear Stromberg cussing and swearing at the damn car alarm, but it worked. He started the engine and burned rubber to get away from the noise. Portia waited a four count, and then doggedly got back on his trail.

The followers hi-fived each other and proceeded to play follow the leader.

Chapter 23

Dinner passed without Billy in attendance. Viv helped out in the restaurant, trying not to be in the way or make the staff feel threatened by her help. But she couldn't just sit still. Her meal was great, but it would have been better with Billy sitting there with her. No doubt and no hiding the fact that there was something between them. Momma and Dad noticed it all.

As Dad turned the "open" sign over, Billy pulled into the parking lot. "He's home!" His voice boomed through the empty restaurant. Momma and Vivika got to the front at the same time.

"Do we miss him, or does he have us trained?" Vivika asked Momma. They both chuckled.

Billy only made it one step inside the restaurant. "Are you hungry?" "How are you?" "What did they find?" "Come sit. Tell us everything!" A chorus of three anxiously awaiting full grown kids.

Momma went to the kitchen and brought a platter out from the oven. She had set aside dinner for her son. Vivika retrieved a pitcher of iced tea and a full glass of ice. His Dad brought out two bottles of ice cold beer and sat them on the table.

He sat and rubbed his scalp with both hands. Viv walked around behind him and without asking started kneading his neck and shoulders. Momma put the platter down in front of him and Dad handed him one of the beers.

"Nothing was found that would confirm it's the sniper, but there's zero chance that it's someone else. It's him."

"Son, are you in any danger? I mean immediate danger?" Dad asked.

"It's pretty serious. If he could spend that much time doing all of that to my car and no one saw him do it? This guy's pretty dangerous." He took a long draw on the beer and picked up a fork.

"What is your supervisor going to do about this?" Momma asked.

"What can he do? Admin leave with pay? This guy has been doing this for what, seven months? I hide out for a couple of days or weeks and, poof, he shows up?" He took a bite of food.

Viv kept on with her massage. "So this was some sort of warning?" She asked.

"Yes. We found 'leave me alone' written in dust on the hood of the car. And I found a sprig of mesquite on the trunk and on the ground. Same size and age as I tracked him in last night." He took another bite of food, and washed it down with a gulp of beer.

Viv stopped rubbing, and Momma covered her mouth at the details. Dad lowered his head. Billy sensed the dread. "Okay enough of this bullshit,"

"Billy!" Momma scolded him.

"Mom, I'm tired." He reached up and took Viv by the hand. He pulled her around in front of him and she found a chair. "How was the rest of your afternoon and evening? Did the folks drive you crazy?" He laid his fork down and scooted the beer away from his hand.

"They were fine. I ate, I bussed tables. I have to pay for my room and board somehow." She winked at Momma.

"Billy I've never met anyone like her. I think Vivika talked Edith into selling that dump to her." Dad stated flatly.

"She, you what?" Billy pushed himself back in his chair.

"We stopped and I asked her if she was thinking about retiring and if she was, to give me a call. Nothing special." She reached for his beer, took a small swig, made a sour face, and put the bottle back down.

"Great, now you've got girl germs on the bottle!" Dad made fun of them both.

"You want to buy that place?" Billy still didn't believe what he had just heard.

"A girl's got to live someplace, and why not make some money at the same time." Viv said with a smile.

"But." Stymied, Billy wasn't sure what to say. As bone tired as he was, he processed the situation. They weren't married. Were they even boyfriend-girlfriend yet? He didn't know much about her recent history, other than the National Tab story.

"I guess I should put everything on the table. I trust each of you with all my heart." Everyone's attention to her intensified. "You all know about the accident. You've read the article and seen the pictures. But what is not in that article are two or three little-known facts. One, I haven't been back to Seattle in almost two years. I left there in search of something. What or who, I don't know. Second, I have amnesia. I don't remember anything about my life prior to the accident. Apparently, I was a pretty good gymnast. Lots of winning and awards over the years. I also found out that, somehow, I was married to the coach of the gym. I have only one friend in Seattle. She was my physical therapist after my accident. She writes me letters constantly, but I haven't answered a single one, and I haven't called her. The only person that knows my whereabouts is my attorney."

"Honey, you don't have to tell us any of this." Momma put her hand on Viv's. "I think we all love you as you are right now." Billy was hesitant, but they all nodded in agreement.

"No, I think you need to know as much as I do about who is living with you."

"It's ok, Vivika. You share as much as you need to." Dad's comforting voice washed over her.

"After the accident there was a huge cash settlement, with monthly payments. I also have lifetime health care. Before I left Seattle, my friend Portia and I were able to piece together some background on me. She brought the medical file to my house and we went through it page by page. Those pictures in the National Tab came from that file."

"She sold the pictures to the tabloid?" Instantly pissed off, Dad raged. "I'll kick her ass if I ever see her!"

"I can't imagine she would do that. But in the file, there were also memos from a private investigation into my history. The coach was suspected of molestation, not just me, but others as well. But they couldn't prove anything."

Dad stood up, knocking his chair backwards onto the floor.

"Robert! Please!" Momma pleaded for calm.

"From all indications, I ran the gym and he stole from a trust fund that had been set up after my parents died in a plane crash. So, I have some business experience."

"But Viv, that place needs to be bulldozed and started fresh from scratch." Billy advised.

"That's sort of how I feel about myself, or did. I think we can both use a second chance or a fresh start-from scratch." A tear rolled down her cheek.

"It's agreed then. If Edith sells, we'll help you anyway we can. And you can stay with us as long as it takes. Consider this your home." Dad spoke; no one blinked or offered any input. He got up from the table and got another beer.

"Even if the place doesn't make money,

I'll be fine." Viv said.

"Then we need to hear from Edith before we go any further. And if she won't sell, we'll find you another place." Momma spoke with authority. Again, no one offered any input. "And now it's late, time for bed. Look at poor Billy. He can't even keep his eyes open." She was right. Even as the important discussion took place, the poor man was drifting in and out.

"Billy, you'll stay here tonight. I don't want you out on the road. No arguments. Your room is still right back there." Momma pointed toward the back of the restaurant.

"Fine." He was in no shape to argue.

The four of them stood up at the same time. Momma figured it out first. She hugged and gave Viv a smooch on the cheek. Father and son said their goodnights, mother and son, Dad and Viv.

Viv started giggling, "This is silly! Goodnight everyone." Everyone agreed but Billy.

"I didn't get a hug from Viv and I'm not going to bed until I get one!" Billy stomped his foot and smiled. Momma and Dad froze.

"Let me go get you a pillow." Viv said, laughing as she walked away. Momma and Dad turned and looked at each other as if to say, "Wow, she won't take his shit, will she?" They laughed.

"Son, looks like you're on your own." Dad said.

Billy stood his ground, and waited. He

could see Viv trying to hide around the corner at the kitchen doorway.

"Ok ok, ya big baby." Viv came back around the corner.

The front window of the restaurant exploded as a huge chunk of plaster blew off the wall just above Viv's head.

"GET ON THE FLOOR NOW!!!" Billy screamed. "Everybody stay still, don't move." He withdrew his weapon from its holster and low-crawled to the front door.

"Billy, what's going on?" Viv called to him.

"It's the same guy from the grocery store. Take my cell and call 911." He slid it across the floor toward the booth. "Stay down, but everyone get over here under this big booth. Dad, lay the table down in front of you guys. Now!" He opened the front door as a distraction for the trio to take cover. Billy took a deep breath, slipped outside, and took cover in front of his car, looking around, breathlessly waiting for another shot. After 9:00 pm in the off season, the main street of Elephant Butte was cemetery quiet. No sounds, no passing cars, and no second shot.

Not long after Viv called 911, the creepy quiet of the night turned to chaos. Law enforcement vehicles from every corner of the county started showing up in the parking lot of the restaurant. Guns drawn, yelling, taking cover, taking stock of the situation via rushed conversations, radio chatter, a repeat of the last two days. Billy was fed up. His boss was chapped. Momma, Dad, and Viv were scared for Billy and themselves.

Chapter 24

The good Attorney Henderson made two calls at the same time the restaurant was under attack. The first call was to Viv, but for the tenth time in as many days he got her voice mail, and again he left a singular message, "Miss Stryker, this is Mr. Henderson. Call me as soon as you get this message. It's urgent I speak with you."

His second call that evening was to the man in black. "Goodblood, this is Henderson. Give me a call about our mutual client. A--sap."

* * * * *

Portia one eye barely open. The other had been doing its own thing for the last two hundred miles. That one eye took casual note of the green highway sign:

Truth or Consequences 2 miles.

"Come on perv, stop to pee or pass out for a couple of hours." She was coaching the coach from a mile behind him, in her own car. "Gas? Food? Something, you freak! Just stop and give me a break!"

In the distance, she spotted a faint blinking red light. A turn signal? He was turning off? "Thank you!!!" She shouted.

Behind her, the followers smiled at each other. "Do you think she has any idea her road trip is over?"

"Nah. But the fun has just started." They kept driving, following the two cars.

* * * * *

"Henderson, Goodblood here, what's up?" The man in black returned Henderson's phone call.

"I'm getting worried. I just left her another voice mail. It's not like her. One or two messages at the most."

"I'm sure something will turn up in the next twelve hours, twenty-four at the most." The tone of his voice was comforting but Henderson he wanted more. He wanted proof the client was alive and well.

"Call me the instant you find out. Please."

"You know I will. Bye." Goodblood was finished with his phone call.

* * * * *

Coach Stromberg pulled off at the same off ramp that Vivika had a few days before, made the left turn, and a hundred yards or so, pulled into the same hotel parking lot that Officer Montez had escorted her into. He checked in.

Portia waited in the parking lot and watched Stromberg, shocked he actually checked in. He pulled his car in front of room 114, got out, and took his bag inside. She put on one wig that she'd held back, one that the coach hadn't seen yet, *if* he'd seen any of the others. And she checked in, asking if room 113 was available. Yes, but it was a smoking room, king with an in-room hot tub, and it was... She cut the night manager off in mid-word, "I'll take it."

After Portia checked in, she parked near her room. The followers did the same. Checked in, parked near their room, and crashed for however long before Stromberg went looking for his child bride.

Chapter 25

"The round came through the front window and slammed into the wall. None of you heard the shot from outside?"

The four of them nodded that they had not heard a sound from outside, just the shattering glass and the thud of the bullet hitting the wall.

"From the looks of it, that round had a very flat trajectory." Billy's supervisor stepped up on a chair and slipped his pen into the bullet hole. "Look at that, damn near straight in. Slightly upward, but damn near flat." He got down from the chair, went outside and spoke with a few officers, then came back in and got back on the chair. This time he had a laser pointer. He inserted one end into the bullet hole, clicked the button, and the red laser beam shot out into the night. "Anything?" He hollered to the officers outside.

"Nothing." He answered.

He adjusted his aim with the laser. "Follow it from the ground out." The red beam started on the parking lot so the officers could track it. Across the parking lot, the street, exactly between two buildings on the opposite side of the street, the beam showed up on a cactus, someone's fence, and then continued into oblivion.

"Okay, that's the direction I want everyone moving. Get on it." His booming voice commanded his men into action.

Billy started out the front door. Tracking was his forte'.

"Where the hell are you going, Montez?" His boss asked.

"Back to work."

"I don't think so. You need to be with your family and girlfriend. You all should think about spending the night, or the rest of the week for that matter, somewhere else."

"Why? He can find us anywhere. Besides, the living quarters were an add-on fifty years ago. The walls are over a foot thick. We'll be safe back there."

"I'll take the first watch." Robert Montez said. "Billy, take your mom and Vivika into the house."

Billy took his mom and Vivika to the back of the restaurant into the living quarters as instructed. "I think we should all stay in the same room, away from the windows. We'll put as many walls as we can between us and the outside."

There were office buildings on both sides of the restaurant and, to the rear, a boat storage yard. The only real vulnerable area of the restaurant layout was to the front, and the sniper had exploited that angle. Billy made sure all the windows and doors were locked, and all of the drapes pulled tight. The living room was the largest room. With a couple of recliners and a huge L-shaped sectional sofa, they would have a safe haven for the rest of the night.

Dad left the cops at the front of the restaurant and went to a closet in a back bedroom. He brought out his old shotgun, loaded. He intended to stand watch, fully prepared to defend his life, home, and loved ones.

Billy's boss decided that there wasn't much else they could do for the night and leaving a cop at the scene was a waste of good manpower. He called a halt to the investigation for the night, he wished Robert good luck, and left.

Dad pulled a chair over into a dark corner of the restaurant, sat down with the shotgun across his lap, a cup of coffee next to him. He was ready for the long night.

Billy helped with blankets and pillows for the recliners and sofa. His mom chose a recliner, the shock of the window exploding and what it really meant settling in on her. Billy was in grave danger. She started to tremble. Billy wrapped his mom up in two blankets, tucked her in, and kissed her forehead goodnight.

Viv was worried about Momma and told Billy as much. He held up a finger in a minor ah-ha moment. He pulled the recliner closer to the sofa, sat down on the couch and motioned for Viv to join him. She brought two blankets from the other end of the sofa, snuggled in tight to Billy, and pulled a blanket over them. Billy reached a few inches and took his mother's hand in his, squeezing. They were all asleep in minutes.

"Dahling, this is the way it should be, forever."
"Kid you've found a keeper."
"Bullet bullet, you met the man with a bullet."

*   *   *   *   *

Momma was the first to awake and get up. She stood and gazed down at Billy and Vivika, spooning on the sofa. Her heart sang. She started to clap her hands, but thought better of it and let the couple sleep. She crept out of the living quarters and into where Dad still sat in the corner with his shotgun and coffee. He was wide awake.

"We made it through the night, Momma." He smiled.

"My brave man kept us safe." She bent and kissed him. "You're going to need to sleep soon. I'll make some breakfast."

"I'm going to keep the restaurant closed today."

"That's fine. We need to get this mess cleaned up. Call Carlos to come replace that window."

"Carlos? He's the one with that old beat up white van?"

"That's the one. You should see Billy and Vivika on the sofa." She smiled and gave a heavy happy sigh.

The crunch of gravel made them both lurch. "Get back in the house." Dad ordered, standing up with the shotgun. The sun was heading higher in the sky, and it was almost broad daylight.

A few locals banded together and commuted to the restaurant to lend their moral and physical support in the aftermath of the shooting the night before. Two SUV's loaded with neighbors, friends and other local business owners pulled up to the restaurant.

Dad moved to the door and peeked outside. Immediately recognizing the group of people. He set the shotgun down, and shouted the all clear to Momma.

Billy heard the gravel and voices. He gingerly left Vivika on the couch, covered with a blanket, and went to confirm his hunch of what was going on outside, checking his weapon as he moved through the house into the restaurant.

Carlos, in his beat-up van, showed up a few minutes later than the main group of well wishers and a couple of busy bodies. Among the visitors were Edith, Marv, and Claudia.

"We heard about the trouble you had last night, and came to lend a hand." Edith elected herself spokesperson.

"I brought you some fresh peaches." Marv said, standing empty handed and leaning on his cane. "They're in the back." He thumbed over his shoulder. "You'll have to have someone get them out. To heavy for me."

"How?" Dad was cut short.

"I heard it on the police scanner. Then

Claudia called me a few minutes later. I drove by here last night, then called everyone and suggested we wait until this morning." Edith said.

"This is great. Thanks everybody. Momma, let's fire up the kitchen, make some coffee for everyone." Dad said.

"We came to help, not create a bigger mess, Robert." Edith protested.

"The kitchen wasn't damaged. How about it Momma? Breakfast on the house for all our friends?" Billy asked.

"Why not, we still have to eat. We'll make a buffet line. I'll go get started." Momma left for the kitchen.

The group moved en masse to the window and peered in at the wall, looking for the bullet hole. The murmuring started in the back and soon they were all commenting and having a grand conversation.

"Billy, was this the work of that gol' dern sniper feller?" Marv asked.

"Pretty sure Marv. Waiting on ballistics to see if the bullet matches the other shootings. Then we'll know for sure."

"Glad you weren't hurt. I need to sit down, rest this hip and knee. It's hell gettin' old Billy." Marv complained. Billy helped the old man to a chair inside the front door.

The group waited for Marv to step aside, and then filed into the room to see the damaged wall up close. More questions about what was heard. Nobody was hurt?

Truth or Consequences

Carlos started work on the window frame, taking the frame apart, brushing the glass aside, and making measurements.

Vivika gently woke up to the sounds of extra footsteps and hushed voices coming from the kitchen. She stretched and went into the kitchen. As she did, she couldn't help but see all the people in the restaurant.

"What's going on?" She asked Momma.

"All of our friends came to check on us and help. We're going to feed them all. How did you sleep?" Momma asked.

"It feels like it was the first time I've ever slept." She stretched again and finished a yawn. "Wow, I feel great."

"Wake up so you can help with breakfast." Dad told Viv jokingly.

"I'm awake. What do you want me to do?" She asked as she washed her hands in the large kitchen sink.

"You don't need to do a thing sweetie." Momma told her and shot Dad a dirty look that changed to a smile.

"That's crazy. Let me crack the eggs. Buffet style right?" Her recently discovered favorite dining style.

"Here are the eggs and a bowl. Start crackin'." Dad said with a smile in his voice.

Billy remained in the front of the restaurant fielding questions. What time did it happen? What caliber was the bullet? He did his best to answer his curious neighbors without giving out critical information not yet available to the public.

"Is your girlfriend here?" Edith asked.

"Ah, Vivika is here. She's staying here with my mom and dad for a while. I'm not sure we are boyfriend and girlfriend." He wasn't sure how to handle the question.

"I wanted to speak with her in private when she gets a chance." Edith said.

"I think she's still asleep. Let me check." He headed into the kitchen first and found Viv cracking eggs into a large bowl. His parents' practiced hustle never ceased to amaze him. They could whip up twenty different orders with just the two of them in the kitchen. Efficiency in every move, no wasted motion.

"Good morning son." Momma spotted him first.

"Good morning everybody." He replied.

Vivika stopped cracking eggs and dodging Momma and Dad. She went to Billy and gave him a hug. "Good morning Officer Montez. Thanks for protecting me all night." She smiled, and then moved back to her eggs.

"When you get a chance, Edith wants to talk to you in private."

Vivika looked at Dad. He winked at her. "You've got her, Viv."

"Ya think?"

"No question. How many eggs did you get cracked?" He asked.

"One whole flat so far."

"That's a good start. Go talk to Edith. I'll take it from here." He grabbed a large whisk as he passed between the grill and the two women.

"You sure?" She started washing her hands.

"Yes, yes, now scoot." Playfully he pointed the wire whisk at her.

Viv walked into the group of supporters. Edith was deep in conversation with Claudia, her body language telling. She wasn't buying anything that Claudia was selling about some gossipy rumor about someone. Marv was holding court from his chair, more like his throne with his cane as his scepter. He recounted a hunting trip from the early 1950's, when it was so cold he froze to the saddle on the trail horse that was taking him to higher ground. Viv walked straight up to Edith. "Good morning Edith."

"Good morning Vivika. You didn't get hurt?" She asked.

"Nope. We're all in one piece."

"Bet you were scared." Claudia sniped.

"Not at all. Billy and Dad wouldn't let anything happen to Momma and me." Viv ground the answer into Claudia.

"Momma and dad, is it?" Claudia said.

"May I talk to you outside, alone?" Edith asked Viv.

"Yep. Nice seeing you again Claudia." Viv walked outside with Edith in tow.

Claudia glared as the pair strolled outside.

Chapter 26

"What do you mean you can't tell me if she's here or not? She's my damn wife!" Stromberg was thundering at Barb, the hotel day manager.

"Even if I wanted to tell you! You're being an ass! Now leave my office!" Barb stood her ground.

"Listen, you-"

"Is there a problem here?" One of the followers that checked in the night before was behind Coach Stromberg.

"What's it to you?" Stromberg said to the stranger.

"I could hear you all the way outside. Figured there was some major problem in here." He looked into Barb's eyes. She knew the look and stepped back from the counter.

"Look asshole." Stromberg barked.

"No need for name calling." The follower said.

"I asked you to leave. Now leave or I'll call the police." Barb said.

"I think this nice man is ready to leave." The follower said.

"And just what the hell makes you think I'm going to leave without finding out about my wife?" Stromberg squared off with the other man.

The follower, so fluid and fast that Barb never saw the actual move, he ran his right hand

Truth or Consequences

over Stromberg's left forearm, then under the forearm. Grasping the coach's fingers with his right hand and pulled down and back. "Ready to walk outside?" He never raised his voice to the coach.

"Don't break my arm!!!" Stromberg shrieked, and went limp, almost touching the ground with his left knee.

"You ready?" He asked Stromberg again.

"YES!!!"

"Thought so." The follower turned to look at the name tag of the clerk, "Barb, is it? If he gives you any more trouble, let me know. I have a hunch he won't be a bother. Isn't that right?" He turned and the coach was forced to follow his every move, as if they were stuck together with Velcro.

"No problems, no nothing, just don't break my wrist!" Stromberg whimpered.

Barb waved a silent thank you grateful to see them go.

The follower took Stromberg out into the parking lot. "Now, you gonna play nice?" He asked the coach.

"Hell yeah, yes, no trouble mister."

"Ok." He released the wrist lock on the coach. "Have a nice day." Walking away, he turned and looked at the coach, then got into the waiting car with his partner and left. Portia was their target. He only stopped when he overheard the coach bellowing from the office. He'd done his good deed for the hour. The follower loved eating bullies for breakfast, but now they had to get back on Portia's trail. She had left early in the morning. They surmised she was up and left early for breakfast, figuring the coach would sleep in. The small GPS transmitter they surreptitiously put under the bumper of her car was showing up perfectly on the laptop in the front seat of the followers' highly modified vehicle. The signal from her car indicated she was about a mile from their location. They proceeded in that direction.

    Coach Stromberg licked his wounded ego and returned to his room. He sat on the bed reviewing the FedEx receipt. This was the hotel. She *was* here, but now, who knew? She could have received the package and left town again. Something nagged at him. His inexplicable hunch told him she was close by. He flipped back through the entire file. Receipts, phone bills, financial statements, bill of sale for an SUV, credit card applications, expenses, hand written notes to Henderson about nothing of import. "Whoa whoa whoa," He thumbed back through the documents. "Bill of sale?" The details of what she should be driving were in his shaking hands. He needed a drink. Her cell phone number was there in plain sight, but what good would that do him? If he called her, it would tip her off that he had at least that much information on her. But he had the make and model of her car, plus the out of state license plate number, "If she's still in town, I got the bitch." He re-filled his travel mug and chug a lugged the leftovers in the bottle for his breakfast.

The followers found Portia's car parked outside of a florid restaurant with five-foot tall letters in brilliant red, telling travelers the joint was open for breakfast seven days a week at 5 am. They pulled into the parking lot and parked to the right of the front door. She hadn't spotted them tailing her for 1500 miles, because she was focused on the car she was following, but they parked out of a direct line of sight just in case.

The follower who had settled the run-in at the hotel went in to order two coffees and get a visual on Portia. She was sitting to the left of the front door near a huge bank of windows. He ordered two large coffees, black, to go. He read the headlines on the local newspaper hanging in a rack by the cashier. An unobserved observer, he noticed Portia had a glass of water, a glass of iced tea, and a runt sized glass of tomato juice. She was waiting for her breakfast. A waitress put two cups of coffee down next to the cashier and as the cashier asked for the $5.43 for the coffee, a different waitress carried a serving tray to Portia's table. He paid the cashier, took the coffees in hand, and stopped at Portia's table. Her breakfast plate was piled high with rich golden hash browns, three slices of bacon, three link sausages, and an omelet that hung off both sides of the plate.

"I hope you're not going to eat that all by yourself?" He said with a grin.

She paused with the first fork full of

omelet halfway to her mouth, quickly sized up the intruder. Perfect haircut, form fitting brown leather bomber jacket, black pants-with cuffs no less. Industrial strength shoes, also black. And not a local. Teeth and smile way too perfect, and a complexion that didn't yell out years of bright sunshine and 10% humidity. His skin looked baby butt perfect. There were several scars: over his left eyebrow, right cheek and two side by side on his chin.

"I'm going to do the best I can." She smiled.

"What's in the omelet?"

"The waitress said everything but the kitchen sink. It's the house special." She noticed his hands. Beefy.

"I'll have to try that the next time I come in. Enjoy! Sorry for bothering you." He turned and left without giving her a chance to comment further.

In case she was watching, the followers pulled out of the parking lot and retreated to an abandoned gas station across the street. The rusty gas price sign showed the last price of gas was $1.22. They backed up into the shade of the building, and sipped their coffees. "They've got a great looking omelet on the menu." Bomber Jacket informed his partner.

"That's nice."

Silence prevailed as they worked on the coffee. Twelve minutes passed. "Look who's here."

"Ah shit. Pull back over there. I guess I'll have an omelet too."

Stromberg parked his car crooked three parking spaces from Portia's car. He was already toasted from the vodka. He wouldn't have recognized Portia if she opened the door and took his order.

The followers pulled back into the parking lot to their original position. Bomber Jacket walked back into the restaurant and the waitress said sit anywhere. Stromberg settled for the table furthest from the front door, with his back to the other patrons.

Bomber jacket walked past Portia's table and hesitated, "I had to come back and try that omelet. Is it as good as it looks?"

"A little heavy on the grease, but it docs have everything but the kitchen sink." She smiled, then dabbed her lips with a napkin.

"Oh well, I'm still going to order it. Thanks." He nodded a good day to her and took a seat in the next booth, facing her.

She was nearly done with her breakfast. With her back to the front door, she never saw Stromberg come in. His waitress came and took his order, and the waitress passing Portia's table asked if she was done with her plate. Yes. She took the plate on her way to the kitchen window. Portia sat with her full tummy and sipped the iced tea, trying very hard not to stare at her breakfast buddy. He absorbed her stare and returned one of his own.

There was a clattering of silverware and a glass crashing on the floor from the area where Stromberg sat. Cussing ensued, but was inaudible. Then the cussing and swearing got louder as Stromberg stomped his way toward the restroom, a few feet on the other side of where Bomber Jacket sat, who watched as Stromberg came mumbling and cussing, rubbing and dabbing a napkin over the crotch of his sweat pants. Apparently he had spilled his beverage of choice on his lap.

Bomber Jacket and Stromberg locked eyes, and that's what Bomber Jacket wanted, to keep the man's focus on him and off Portia.

As Stromberg passed Portia's table, she recognized his voice and bulk. She slunk down in the booth and turned her head to the window.

Stromberg kept moving to the restroom.

As soon as the bathroom door closed, Portia was on the move. She hurried to the cashier, laid a twenty and a five on the counter and instructed: "Keep the change." She was out the front door and into her car before Bomber Jacket could inhale.

He flagged down his waitress. "I need my order to go, please."

Portia left the parking lot in a silent flurry.

It took another seven minutes for Bomber Jacket's order to show up in a white Styrofoam to-go box. He paid the cashier, and met up with his partner in the car. "What's up?"

"She left almost ten minutes ago. Check

the GPS tracker."

Chapter 27

"Vivika were you serious about buying my business?" Edith stood facing Vivika outside the restaurant.

"Very serious."

"Make me an offer."

"Hey kid, first one to name a number loses."

"What's it worth to you?" Vivika listened to Grumpy.

"It's worth about a hundred and fifty." Edith ventured. It might be worth that much in a good economy, with that much put into remodeling.

Viv twisted her mouth. Looked away for a couple of beats. "I was thinking less than that. Remember, I'm offering you cash. No banks, no bullshit. Try another number."

"Outstanding, kid!"

Edith thought of the second and third price she'd come up with overnight. She thought of Bill and his health. "A hundred grand and it's yours." Hopeful, she let the words fall as they may. She had one more number if Viv balked at this one.

Viv thought it over, waiting for input from Grumpy.

"Fifty in cash. The rest in payments."

"How about this. You need to be closer to the doctors in Las Cruces for Bill. I don't know if you two have Social Security coming in or not, but it seems to me you need a lump sum to hit the road, get set up in a new home, and what not, then what? Then you'll have no monthly income from the business, so what next?"

"Wonder what's going on with those two?" Claudia said aloud, staring intently at the pair just outside the window and earshot.

"Edith, think about this last offer. Fifty thousand in cash tomorrow and two grand a month for a couple of years until the balance is paid off." Vivika laid it all out.

Edith's knees weakened. She felt faint. Bill would faint dead away if she sold the business like this. He'd love it. She loved it. Edith backed up against one of the SUVs. "Whew."

"You need a minute?" Viv asked.

"More like a shot of tequila and a chair."

"I can get that for you. Hang on." Viv headed inside.

She quickly grabbed a bottle of tequila, two shot glasses, and a wooden chair and went back outside to Edith. Viv helped her to the chair, handed her both shot glasses, and poured the amber bliss into the shot glasses.

"You've got a deal!" Edith raised her glass.

"Great!" Viv raised and clinked her glass to Edith's. The deal was done.

Edith began to cry. "I gave up hope of ever leaving that place alive." Her sobbing intensified.

"Ohhh." Viv lowered herself to Edith's side. "It'll be okay now. And if you need more money, I can hire you back as a consultant!" She hugged her new friend as tightly as she could. She felt Edith shake as she took in deep breaths, trying to stem her tears.

They stayed in the hug.

"Something major just happened between those two." Claudia spouted off, bringing everyone in the dining room to attention. Everyone stopped talking and stared.

"Why don't you come inside and I'll buy you an iced tea?" Viv said.

"How about another shot of tequila?" Edith proffered.

"We can do that too!" Viv giggled and poured them another round.

Robert heard Claudia's big mouth and then the silence. He walked out of the kitchen, saw Viv and Edith toasting with tequila and knew what it was all about. "Claudia, I need a hand in the kitchen. Care to help out?"

"Sure Robert." She almost ran into the door frame going into the kitchen, her neck twisted to watch the two women outside.

The rest of the crowd went back to their cliques and conversations. They could care less about Viv and Edith.

"How are we going to do this?" Edith asked.

"Do what?"

"The sale. If you want to do a cash only deal, we need to do it right hon."

"Oh, hmm. I'll call my attorney and have him fly down here and handle the paperwork. Should be easy for him."

"You have an attorney?"

"Long story. There was an accident and a settlement. I'm sure he won't mind taking care of the details for us. Not to worry. When we go in, I'll call him." She held up the bottle to offer another shot, but Edith waved her off. "I have him on speed dial on my cell phone." Viv smiled.

"What are we waiting for?" Edith got up from her chair and headed inside.

Marv was storytelling to a small audience. Claudia had been hijacked to the kitchen. One woman had a broom, and her companion held a dust pan. A man was holding an extension cord, looking for an outlet to hook up to so he could operate the heavy duty vacuum cleaner. A couple of men were wiping glass from table tops. The chit chat had died off and the work they came to do was getting underway.

Viv followed Edith into the kitchen. "Robert." Edith called out.

"Yes Edith?" He turned from the grill with a spatula in one hand and a burger press in the other.

"I hope Billy doesn't let this little thing get away from him. She's a winner." Edith proclaimed, embarrassing Viv.

"I know just how you feel." He replied

and winked at Viv. "I hope you're hungry Edith?" Robert turned back to the grill and scooped and shuffled the mound of hash browns in the hot glistening grease.

"I'm so excited! Not sure I can eat right now."

Robert looked back at her, "You made a sale, I take it?"

Claudia stopped peeling potatoes and glared at Edith.

"Damn straight!" Edith walked up behind Robert and slapped him on the back.

"That's fantastic!" Momma congratulated her longtime friend.

"Bill will be well taken care of from here on out." Edith said fighting back tears. Viv slipped an arm around Edith's waist and squeezed her in support.

"I guess I'll go make my phone call." Viv excused herself to go fetch her cell phone. She got to *her* room, and grabbed her bag. It wasn't a pocket book and not really a purse either. It was a large bag. The first thing she noticed was the aroma of a half eaten bag of Corn Nuts. She took a deep whiff and set them aside. Scrounging around in the darkness of the bag, she pulled out a handful of receipts she probably should send to Mr. Henderson. Her wallet came out and set aside. Three minutes of dragging the contents to one side then the other, Viv had had enough and dumped the entire bag onto her bed. No cell phone. She crammed everything back into the

Truth or Consequences

bag, stood back with her hands on her hips and thought about the last place she used the stupid thing? Ah hah! Her car of course. She went out the back door to the side of the restaurant, where she was told to park it. Not on the dashboard, not in the center console, not on the floorboard. She looked down the side of the seat next to the console, under her seat. Where the hell is it? She opened the hatch and checked in her two suitcases. It was nowhere to be found.

"All right you guys, where's my damn phone?"

"At the hotel. Damn kid all you had to do was ask."

"No shit. Thanks Grumpy."

"Vivika!!" Robert called out for her.

"I'm out here!" She answered him.

"Breakfast is ready!"

"I'll be right there." She headed for the breakfast line.

*   *   *   *   *

The starched and ironed uniform felt oddly confining to Billy. He couldn't remember the last time he had been out of uniform for three days straight. The material was scratchy sliding over his skin, but he still liked what he saw in the mirror as he checked that his tie was straight. From head to toe, he was a sharp looking guy and the uniform was the icing. He laughed at his personal review.

Back on patrol. Anderson called in sick, suspected Swine Flu. Billy had hoped to get another full day with Vivika, now it would be four straight days on the job, then off one, then back on the job for two, on and on, but Vivika was his light at the end of the tunnel and the thought of her would sustain him on the long boring beat. Maybe there would be some forensics movement on the sniper. Hopefully, Vivika wouldn't be bored to death by his parents, and what was up with her buying Bill and Edith's janky ass place? So many distracting thoughts as he left the locker room of the Central District Offices of the State Highway Patrol. Signed in, signed out, he carried his day-bag to his patrol unit. He performed his check list of the unit: flares, emergency blankets and yellow tarps, rifle, shotgun, ammo, tires were in good shape, lights and sirens in fine working order. Time to hit the road. Wonder what Vivika will do today? He drove out of the high security fenced parking lot.

Officer Billy Montez headed south on I-25 from the station house. He tailed a farmer and his old beat up flatbed truck, overweight with sacks of grain. The old guy was heading back to his little farm up in the hills. He let him go on with his day, no ticket. Billy pulled off I-25 and made a pass through the little hot pepper town of Hatch. Too early on a weekday for much action. School was in session, farm workers were dispersed out into the thousands of acres of pepper farms, busy with their own day's work.

Truth or Consequences

The streets were quiet and empty. On the other end of town, he pulled back onto I-25 south and headed for his turnaround spot at the Port of Entry checkpoint.

Again, he thought of Vivika. She would be eating breakfast with Momma and Dad, and whoever showed up at the restaurant. I think I love her. He shook his head in disbelief. No way can you love her, you barely know her. "There are no routine stops." His instructors' voices pushed their way passed titillating thoughts of Vivika. "Stay focused, no distractions." It takes two seconds to pull a trigger three times. A fleeting moment of distraction, and a flag draped coffin could be the result." He did his best to wall off his vision of Vivika.

Officer Montez pulled his patrol car into the shadow of an overpass, facing north. The passing traffic wouldn't see him until it was to late. Their speed would already appear on his radar gun. The first speeder, clocked at 92 mph, was written a ticket for 85 in a 75 mph zone. The second speeder faced a harsher ticket. The driver failed the attitude test and Officer Montez spent fifteen minutes writing up the ticket: 87 in a 75 mph zone, not wearing a seat belt, bald tires, and expired tags. He took his time finishing up the ticket. "Attitude is key when you get pulled over," he said under his breath, "to bad for you."

A few more tickets and it was time for his morning break. He passed Truth or Consequences heading for the north end of his patrol, and now he was ten miles from passing the town again, heading south. A call came over the radio of a single vehicle accident at the same time he spotted the accident. Ed Hardy, a local rancher, had a blowout on a front tire of his pickup. He had hit the brakes and it spun him out and threw him off the shoulder. The truck had stopped short of rolling over in an arroyo. Ed, shaken up but otherwise fine, made the distress call and was sitting on the side of the highway when Billy rolled up on scene.

"You okay Ed?" Billy asked his fellow townsfolk.

"Oh hell yes. I don't know what I was thinking of. I hit them brakes and I'll be damned the next thing I know I'm sitting down there at the bottom of the hill. Shee-it. I know better. Been driving since I was a ten year old." He shook his head in disgust.

Billy walked down to Ed's truck. The left front tire was shredded from the blowout, and the windshield was cracked from the twisting of the truck frame as it rumbled down the embankment. But to Billy's eye, the truck was probably still drivable. No fluids leaking, no obvious major damage. He headed back up the embankment. "Ed, we'll get you towed out of there, change the tire, and you should be able to drive it home or to town and have someone check it out. But, I'll be shocked if you can't drive it away once we get the tire changed. Just catch your breath now while I get that tow truck started for you."

Truth or Consequences

Once the tow truck was on its way, Billy watched Ed sit shaking his head, calling himself everything he could think of. A one-man ass chewing ensued. Billy laughed it off and waited in his patrol car for the tow truck as he started the paperwork. An uneventful, easy shift so far, three hours into the day. He picked up his cell phone and called his Dad to check in on the restaurant repair.

"Morning son." Dad's phone had caller ID.

"Hey Dad. How're things this morning?"

"Busy. We had some surprise visitors for breakfast."

"You're not open for breakfast." Billy pointed out.

"Tell me about it. Two carloads of people showed up to check on me and your mother. Edith, Claudia, Marv, a bunch of them. Even Carlos the glass man showed up."

"That's great Dad. So, you and Momma fixed them all breakfast?"

"*Vivika,* Momma, and me fixed a breakfast buffet. Some of them helped clean up the glass and what not." Dad said.

"Vivika helped?"

"Worked on the scrambled eggs." He played with Billy, knowing he'd really only called to find out about Vivika.

Billy smiled. "So... what else is going on?" He was pushing a noodle to get the information.

"Not much. Breakfast is done and over. We're closed for the rest of the day."

Billy wanted to shout: What about Vivika?

"The people have cleared out. It's just me and Momma here. I think I'll take a nap."

Sleep all day, but what about Vivika? He bit his tongue. Disrespecting his Dad would only lead to more stalling and build up.

"Oh, there was one other thing that happened this morning." Dad said.

"Yeah, what was that Dad?"

"Edith sold her place to our Vivika."

"No shit!! She's staying!!!"

"Yep. Which means our Vivika will be staying with us for at least six more months while she remodels that dump." Dad was smiling too.

"That's..."

"Fantastic is the word you're looking for son." Still smiling.

"Ok, Dad. Fantastic is a great word. I gotta get back to work. We'll talk some more later."

"Good deal son. Be careful out there."

"Will do. Bye Dad." Beaming with hope, his imagination running wild, Billy could hardly write the date on the paperwork on his clipboard.

When the tow truck arrived, Billy laid the paperwork to one side and got out to talk with Mark Gandy, owner-operator of TRC Towing.

"Afternoon Officer Montez, you fall asleep? I've been here ten minutes."

"Afternoon?" Billy checked his watch, damn that was a fast four hours. "Sorry about that. I was doing the paperwork."

"I know that look." Mark said.

"What look?"

"What's her name?" Mark asked. They had known each other almost twenty years.

"No, no, it's nothing like that. I was just deep in thought about the shooting at the restaurant last night."

"Riiiiight. I would have come over last night, but I was way the hell up passed Socorro on a recovery. Are your folks alright?" He was at the back of his tow truck pulling out the winch cable.

"Yeah, everyone is fine. Scared the hell out of them."

"I'll bet. You guys ever gonna catch this guy?" Mark grabbed two heavy hooks with chains attached off the back deck of the tow truck, and with the winch cable in hand, headed over the side of the embankment toward Ed's truck.

"I hope soon!" Billy admired Mark's skill at all things towing. The crawling in mud, snow, sand and weeds, risking run-ins with snakes and spiders, all with a smile and a grunt. He watched from a distance as Mark hit the ground with the tow hooks, found two secure places under the back of the truck to grab onto, stretched out the chains to the winch cable, and called out to Billy.

"Hey Barney Fife, make yourself useful,

and take the slack out of the chains for me."

Billy walked over to the back of the tow truck and pulled back on a lever with a red knob that engaged the winch. The cable slowly tracked into the hole to the winch spool. Mark walked back up the embankment to his tow truck and took over the winch controls from Billy.

"If you ever need a *real* job Barney, call me."

"Up yours." They laughed at each other.

"So, you're not going to tell me her name, huh?" Mark spoke up over the strain of the winch.

"You don't know her."

"I knew it!" Mark smiled.

"She's not from around here. But looks like she'll be staying for a while." Billy couldn't hide his enthusiasm.

"Uh, oh, you're in love, Billy Montez!" Mark said as he watched Ed's truck buck and struggle to come up the embankment.

"Maybe?"

Ed stood up, brushed off his pants, and walked over to where Billy and Mark were standing, watching his faithful old pickup being dragged up the slope.

The bear-sized Mark hopped into the cab of the tow truck and eased it forward. Ed's truck fell in line and came to a rest facing the wrong way on the shoulder, on flat ground.

"Jump in and see if it will start." Billy said to Ed. He did and the truck started right up.

"Great. Mark'll change the tire for you and you'll be on your way Ed."

"Thanks Billy." Ed stuck out his old calloused hand and shook Billy's hand.

"Mark you got this?" Meaning changing the tire, and making sure Ed got his truck turned around safely on the highway.

"Yeah, not a big deal. Go see your honey!" Mark chided his old friend.

"Watch it or I'll write your ass up!" Billy laughed as he walked back to his car. After having Ed sign the paperwork he drove off to Truth or Consequences for a long overdue lunch break, tapping the horn twice as he drove away. He smiled as he passed the spot on the shoulder where he had found Vivika a few days ago. He pulled off I-25 at the same offramp he had escorted Vivika off.

Chapter 28

"The boogeyman is back. Skip, skip, skip."

"What boogeyman?" Viv asked the little girl.

"Your bothersome husband dahling."

"No way. How in the..." Viv was driving toward the hotel to check with Barb, to see if her cell phone had been found.

"You'll be fine kid."

"If you say so Grumpy." How nuts was she to be carrying on a conversation with three phantom voices? Was it from the crash? Did she hear voices all her life?

"Dahling, we've been with you forever, get over it."

"But,"

"We used to sing and sing, like a cricket in the spring."

Viv tried to shake them off, to no avail. She drove to the hotel. "But how? Who are you guys?".

"Don't have a clue kid, we just are and we're yours."

"Did I use to believe in ghosts or spirits?"

No answer. She made two more turns. The hotel was on the horizon. "When I don't want to hear you guys, you won't shut up. Now I want answers, and you shut up!" She slugged the steering wheel.

Viv wheeled into the hotel parking lot, unmindful of the two cars in the parking lot with Washington state license plates. If Viv had read one of the letters from Portia, she might have noticed the bright yellow hybrid near the office. The other car looked like any other nondescript four door sedan with dark tinted windows.

Viv pulled right up to the office door and went into the office. Barb was sitting behind the registration desk.

"Hi Barb." Viv greeted her.

"Oh hi..."

"Viv." Reminding Barb.

"We have your cell phone back here."

"You do? That's why I'm here. I couldn't find it anywhere."

"The battery is dead, but it's right here." She turned and took it from a desk drawer and handed it over to Viv.

"Thank you so much. I had a hunch I left it in the room. Cool. Thanks again." She turned to leave.

"Wait. There's something else." Barb said, eyes darting around like it was top secret.

"What?"

"There's a man here looking for you. Says he's your husband."

"Interesting." No fear, no concern, Viv didn't know whose side Barb was on.

"He was in here barking at me. Telling me I'd better tell him where you were or else."

"Sounds like a guy I used to know. Big

guy?"

"Pardon me for saying this, a fat stinky slob. And tall." Barb looked around the office again.

"No problem. I haven't seen him in a couple… a long time. Nice to know he hasn't changed. Ok, I'll keep my eye out for him."

"He's staying here." Barb cringed as she spoke the words.

"Charge him triple the rate! Thanks Barb." Viv left the office.

She got in her car and quickly pulled around to the back of the building, plugging the cell phone into its charger. She had to wait for it to power up. It immediately let her know she had ten new messages. Viv ignored the notification and punched the preset phone number for Attorney Henderson.

"Henderson Law Office, how may I help you?" The receptionist answered.

"This is Vivika Stryker. I need to speak with Mr. Henderson please."

"One moment Miss Stryker."

"Vivika, is that really you?" Henderson asked.

"Hank it's me. Alive and well. How are you?"

"I'm fine. Listen Vivika, if you're still in Truth or Consequences, you need to leave now. Go somewhere else and fast!" His voice full of worry and urgency.

"I know the coach is here somewhere. I

just heard all about it from the hotel manager."

"He's staying at the hotel Vivika. Don't let him see you there."

"How'd you know he was here?" She almost missed what he said.

"It doesn't matter. And Vivika," Henderson toned it down.

"Yes?"

"Your friend Portia is at the same hotel. Room one-thirteen."

"How-"

"It doesn't matter right now. You and Portia should leave that little town right now. Hang on a second."

"Ok."

He put Vivika on hold and dialed the man in the bomber jacket. "Hello Hank-"

"Vivika is at the hotel right now!!!"

"I know. We're keeping an eye on her. Portia is still in her room. The coach is at a diner down the road. All is well here."

"You need to collect the girls and get them the hell out of there! I told Vivika to get Portia and get out of the hotel."

"I'll take that under advisement Hank. But for now, I'll let this play out and keep a close watch on things. Is that all?"

"For what I'm paying you…"

"Ok then, I'll call you when there's any change. Bye." Bomber Jacket ended the call.

"Vivika?"

"Yes Hank, I'm still here."

"You need to go to Portia's room, get her and leave the premises. At least for the rest of the day. Please do this!"

"Ok, that won't be a problem. Now, I need something from you."

"If you promise to get out of there?"

"Yes, I promise."

"What do you need?"

"I'm buying some property for cash and I need you down here to handle the paperwork and some other details."

"I'm not licensed to practice in New Mexico."

"Is that a no?" Vivika bit her lower lip.

"No, not at all. I'll figure it out. How soon?"

"Tomorrow?"

"Tomorrow!!"

"Too soon?"

"Shit." He slipped up. Henderson let fly with a tirade of profanities. "I'm sorry Vivika, tomorrow is out of the question. Let me see if I can rearrange my schedule and call you back. You *will* answer your phone now, right?"

"Absolutely. I promise."

"Fine. You get Portia like you promised, and I promise to get there as soon as I can."

"Thank you so much Hank! Talk to you soon." She could hear him cussing as she ended the call. She put her SUV in drive and pulled around the hotel to stop in front of Room 113. This would be a tough reunion. Dammit, she'd just started reading Portia's letters.

Viv gathered herself, moved to the door and knocked. The curtain next to the door fluttered and the door swung open wide.

"Vivika, my child bride, it's so nice of you to join us." Stromberg stood in the doorway. With a flourish he showed off Portia, tied up on the floor.

"You bastard!!!" Vivika shouted.

He grabbed her by the arm and jerked her off her feet, tossing her so hard she flew over on top of Portia.

"A bonus bitch." Leering at them both. "Vivika you and your lover here are such pains in the ass."

Vivika looked at Portia. She was gagged and tied. A knot was swelling under her left eye.

The hydraulic door closer worked great, it shut the door, allowing Stromberg to catch Vivika before she could do anything. He snatched her up and dragged her to the bathroom. "If you make a sound, I'll kill her." He pointed to Portia on the floor. "Then you. You got that?" She nodded and he backhanded her. He closed the bathroom door and turned to the bed to gather more packing tape to bind Vivika.

Portia was helpless, hardly able to wiggle, much less defend herself or Viv. She began to cry.

Vivika looked around the small hotel bathroom for anything that might help her out in an attack on Stromberg. The only thing that crossed her mind was the chrome bar the shower curtain hung from.

"Use it kid."

"Swing a ling a ding dong. Skip, skip, skip."

She draped her hand over the bar. A deep, familiar feeling shot through her as she put both hands on it. Swing. A rough-edged memory came to her. Uneven bars. Swing. There wasn't much room for momentum but she hung there and more memories came back: a cheering crowd, grip, technique. Swing. Involuntarily her body moved back and forth. She was able to get everything moving in a unified motion. Once, twice, three times. Her feet came up to eye level, then bumped the ceiling. The door knob turned. Stromberg walked into the soles of her shoes. Both of her feet planted squarely on his face, sending him tumbling out of the bathroom and crashing hard into the wall opposite of the bathroom. The shower curtain bar failed twice. It kinked in the middle and the screws stripped out of the wall. She fell hard onto the bathtub. Portia lay in the outer room and could only listen and hope.

"This is taking too long." Bomber Jacket said.

"They haven't seen each other in a couple of years, right? They're just taking their time getting reacquainted." His partner responded.

"I've got that feeling."

"Shit. I hate when that happens. Dog or

cat?"

Bomber Jacket chose "Cat."

"You ready?" The car door opened as he asked the question.

Bomber Jacket went to the right of the door, past the window, and his partner knocked on the door. No response. They exchanged knowing looks. He knocked again. Bomber Jacket moved behind his partner. "Move." and sent a powerful kick, knocking the door off two of its three hinges, flopping it open to one side.

Bomber Jacket stepped over Portia. His partner pulled a black weapon from his waist band and covered Portia with his body, gun trained toward Bomber Jacket.

Stromberg had regained a little of his sight and footing. He tried to stand up as Bomber Jacket put him back on the ground with a knife edge slap of his hand to the windpipe. He turned his attention to Vivika, moaning and trying to regain her footing. Her head had slammed into the tub when she fell. She was dazed, but okay.

"Call nine!" Bomber Jacket yelled to his partner.

"I already did. Is she ok?" He gingerly cut Portia free.

"Bumped her head, but looks fine."

Billy listened to the call. "All available units in the vicinity..."

He was at the stop sign at the bottom of the offramp, and didn't bother to answer the dispatcher. He could see the parking lot of the hotel. He nailed the throttle, lights, and sirens all at the same time. He miscalculated his speed versus the sand covered parking lot. When he applied his brakes, he did a 360 spin before he jammed it into park. He jumped out with his gun drawn as Portia was being led out of the hotel door. Then another man was leading *his* Vivika out. "FREEZE!!! LET THE WOMEN GO!!!" Tossing away all of the training at the academy, he advanced straight at the men, gun leveled at both men.

Billy, only a few feet from the men.

"It's okay Billy, they're good guys." Viv said holding her head and squinting.

"Really, the bad guy is inside." Portia chimed in.

From inside the room, a guttural moan, like an animal in pain, Bomber Jacket pulled a gun from his waist band.

"DROP IT!!!" Billy commanded.

The noises from the room gathered intensity. Bomber moved to the side of the door, Billy side-stepped so he could access the room with a narrow wall for cover. With Billy on one side of the door, Bomber Jacket on the other, Portia and Viv were ushered to safety around the corner of the hotel. Then Stromberg tried to run through the window with the sadly bent curtain rod. He got entangled in the drapes, and the rod caught on one side of the window frame, sending him crashing awkwardly through the window. He rolled and tumbled on the ground, finding Billy's weapon on him as he unwrapped himself from the fabric. Bomber Jacket eased in closer.

"Get back over to the wall!" Billy shouted.

Bomber Jacket held out a thick black leather wallet with a gold and blue NYPD shield, across the bottom a single word, Retired. It was enough for Billy, and he lowered his weapon, holstered it, and immediately pulled his handcuffs from his utility belt.

"Do you mind?" Bomber Jacket held out his hand to take the cuffs from Billy.

"I guess, not." He passed them to Bomber Jacket. "You can still read him his rights of course."

"Of course."

Bomber Jacket dropped a heavy knee into Stromberg's back, and the man jumped and screamed in pain. Bomber Jacket let his right hand fall heavy into his cheek bone, "Stop resisting sir." He smiled up at Billy, and his smile was returned.

The scene at the hotel was under control. Bomber Jacket called Attorney Henderson, explaining everything. Henderson responded that he would be on the next flight out, and please don't lose track of Vivika and Portia. Bomber Jacket hung up on him.

"How the hell did he beat us here?" Bomber's partner asked him.

"He must have gone out the bathroom window at that diner, and drove down here before the three of us left there. He was waiting in her room for her."

"Where's his car?"

"Probably around back." He pointed to the hotel.

"I parked back there when I called Mr. Henderson." Viv added.

"Close call." Bomber Jacket said.

*   *   *   *   *

Stromberg was charged with kidnapping, fraud, and possession of a sawed off shotgun they found in his truck - interstate transportation of an illegal weapon. He would not be harassing anyone for a very long time. Twenty-five to life, a straight fifteen before his first parole hearing, which would come when he was around 62 years old.

Portia, Vivika, Bomber Jacket, his partner and Billy were all questioned late into the day and early evening. All of them ended up, exhausted, at the Montez's restaurant. During the ensuing hours, Vivika did her best to explain her part of the mess, with Portia filling in the blanks. Billy was overwhelmed. Too much input on top of his ongoing sniper case and constant exhaustion, he excused himself to a spare bedroom with a cold bottle of beer in one hand, and Viv's hand in the other.

Henderson arrived in Truth or

Consequences the next morning. Following Viv's directions, he drove his rental car to the family restaurant to meet her. He read over and supervised the signing of each document of the sale. He guided Vivika through the pitfalls of purchasing real estate in New Mexico with cash, and a friend of a friend acted as supervising counsel for the visiting Henderson.

Chapter 29

The day after the sale, Vivika got the shock of her life when Edith showed her around the spa. Several hundred gallons of paint would barely cover the remodel Viv saw in her mind's eye. Edith gave Viv the guided tour, they circled the spa facility twice. Viv made mental notes of the decay as Edith went out a battered wooden side gate, across a vacant lot cluttered with debris from the occasional hard winds-abandoned bicycles, piles of chunked up concrete. "Edith honey, where are we going?"

"I want to show you the rest of the property."

Viv, dumbfounded, wanted clarification. "Excuse me?"

Edith stopped, one hand on her hip. "I've been buying up the properties around the spa for the last twenty years. Two years ago I bought the last parcel I wanted. It's down this way." She started walking again.

"Edith, I'm totally confused. If you have more property, why didn't you ask for more money?"

"Hell if I know. My only concern was Bill and his well being. I'm no fool. I know he only has a few more months, maybe a year to live at most. I want him to be happy and comfortable."

She stopped walking again. "Here it is."

Viv looked back. They walked the length

of the city block and stood on the corner. "Here what is?" She looked at a ramshackle house that should have been scraped off the ground it was dying on.

"You see that street sign down there?" Edith asked pointing north along the sidewalk to the end of the street.

"Yes."

"Now look down that way, the way we came from. See that street sign?" She pointed west, to the other end of the street.

"Yes."

"You bought an entire square city block." Edith smiled.

"But, but." Viv was flabbergasted.

"As things got tight for my neighbors, I bought them out, paid cash for each piece." She stood proud of her accomplishment.

"But why? From what I can see you haven't done anything with it."

"Bill got worse and worse without telling me. We had plans to expand the spa. More parking, a classy little ten room hotel. A café over by the spa. But by the time I found out how bad he was, I sure as hell couldn't expect him to do that much work, and I'll be damned if I would pay some stranger to come and do simple projects for me."

"Dahling I love this woman. She's a genius."

"Score one for our side kid!"

"I agree with you both." Viv said.

"What's that hon?" Edith asked.

"Oh I'm just talking to my self."

"Why not hon? I'm the smartest person I know, therefore, I talk to myself all the damn time!" She laughed.

"So all of this property is," she hesitated, "mine?" Viv asked. She could see the ten room hotel, or cute little cedar log cabins, and a huge waterfall in front of the spa. And why not a little five or six table bistro? Or a wi-fi café?

"Yes ma'am."

"What's the zoning like?" Viv asked.

"It's downtown, zoned for businesses and light industrial."

"What about RV parking or a campground?"

"What's an RV, skip, skip, skip?"

"A simple variance and you'd be all set."

*   *   *   *   *

Six months into Viv's remodel of the hot springs spa, she was taken aback when the general contractor she had hired told her that the "grand opening" would have to be pushed back another four months.

"Oh well kid, better get used to changes."

"How many more changes?" Viv asked.

"Miss Stryker, I can't predict the future, but another six, I mean four months should do it." The contractor replied.

"Oh, I was talking to someone else."

The contractor looked around the office. It was him and her.

"Another four months." Viv looked at the floor. "Have you reviewed your contract lately?"

"Hmm, why?"

"Take a look at it, especially the completion clause. I need to go, got some other things to take care of today. Call me." Viv left his office.

"Dahling I love Mr. Henderson."

"Me too Greta." Viv said.

One of the major *changes* in Viv's world over the previous six months was to quit fighting the voices. She gave each one a name. Greta was the raspy voiced older eastern European woman. Grumpy was the older grandpa sounding man. And the rope skipping little girl she named Rebecca. Viv no longer ignored any of them. Each dropped useful and sometimes lifesaving hints and advice. Why fight them? Apparently they were her life-long friends and advisors. Claim them proudly and move on.

Another change in her life was announced in the local newspaper. Billy proposed to her. An engagement picture, wedding date, and gift registry were published in the T R C Times. No one was surprised with their wedding announcement. They spent every available hour together: working on the remodel, hanging out at Momma and Dad's, hiking the region, trail riding, off-roading, she learned to fish and handle a firearm. They became best friends and fell deeply in love. The wedding date was in about four months. The contractor would just have to deal with the contract. He had agreed to a $500 per day penalty for each day past the agreed upon completion date.

Another happy change was Portia moving to Elephant Butte. Viv offered to set up a physical rehab and therapeutic massage suite to call her own, and Portia jumped at the chance. Plus, she found that New Mexico had reciprocity for her licensure and degrees in kinesiology, bio mechanics, and nutrition. Clients could avail themselves of the mineral hot springs before or after a session with her magic hands. Viv gave her a free hand with the design of her facility. Portia called the eclectic design Wild West modern. Knotty pine and chrome, hardwood floors and sleek dual pane metal framed windows. Her office was detached from the actual spa, so it didn't have to match Viv's remodel too closely.

Changes abounded: she adopted a stray puppy when *her* city block was bulldozed, cleared off and leveled. She applied for and received her variance to add a five space RV park. She did run into some hassles with the sewer system, but that went away when Grumpy suggested calling an engineer in Albuquerque.

All in all, she was pleased with the interior and exterior changes in her life.

Viv's cell phone jingled. The caller ID showed it was Billy calling.

"Hey babe." Viv answered the phone.

"Hey good looking. After my shift, are we still on for our trip to Taos?" Billy asked.

"Absolutely."

"Ok, my shift ends in about two hours."

"Great. See you then."

"Okay. See ya love ya bye."

"See ya love ya bye." She smiled, putting her phone back in her pocket.

"Oh, dahling it's amazing up there. You two kids will have a great time." Greta said.

"He said Taos would blow me away."

"You damn kids are so sweet you make my teeth hurt."

"As if, Grumpy!"

A change she lived for: little romantic getaways with Billy.

Chapter 30

It was dark by the time Billy got back to the station house, changed, and let everyone know, one more time, that he was heading north to Taos with Vivika.

Billy and Viv enjoyed a nice dinner with Momma and Dad before their romantic getaway. Dad as usual took his son aside and asked if he needed a few extra bucks for gas and food. Momma followed Viv into her bedroom to watch her pack.

Dad refused to let Billy or Viv carry her luggage to Billy's new truck parked in front of the restaurant. Dad put the luggage in the extended cab truck, behind the front seats, turned and gave Viv a hug.

Billy's pager and cell phone went off at the same time. The stunned group stood and looked at each other, and then all eyes turned to Billy as he answered his cell phone, "Yes. Same place? Dammit. Yessir, I'll be there in less than fifteen minutes." He hung up, slipped the phone into it's holder on his belt, took a deep breath, "It's the sniper. I have to go."

Dad took Vivika's luggage back out of the truck. They moved away from the truck as Billy quickly left.

*   *   *   *   *

Truth or Consequences

The sunrise, brilliant as it might have been, didn't attract Billy's attention. Another night in the hills tracking the phantom sniper. Again, no clear tracks or signs. The sniper took the native bushes and brushed clear his tracks. Billy was exhausted, and now their departure to Taos was set back by ten hours. He was pissy, chapped about the interruption. His dad met him at the door to the restaurant.

"How'd it go?" Dad asked his drag ass son.

"Same as the last thousand times."

"Bit of an exaggeration don't you think?"

"Feels that way." He grumbled hanging his head looking at the cup of coffee his dad handed him. What's another cup of coffee?

"You'll catch him. You're better at finding him than he is of hiding from you."

"Thanks dad." He ran his hand through his short hair. "Damn I'm tired."

"You can go somewhere closer than Taos." Dad offered.

"Yeah, but Viv is looking forward to Taos."

"She won't mind a change of plans. Trust me."

"I don't know dad. I might call it off for this month. I'm beat. Hey, you going to open for business or just chew on me the rest of the day?" Billy sat staring at the coffee cup.

Dad gave Billy a playful smack to the back of his head as he passed by.

"Careful, I'll have you arrested!"
"You got to find me first."
They both laughed.

Viv was busy in the kitchen with Momma, helping with meal preparations. She never hesitated if there was anything she could do for Momma and Dad. They still wouldn't take a dime for rent, and they frowned on her helping in the front of the restaurant, not because she was bad at it, but because the other staff groused too much and too often when she worked the floor.

Viv checked the time, "Ok Momma, I'm going to get my haircut. I think you can handle this."

"Oh you." Momma flicked some chopped lettuce her way.

"I'll be back later today."

Momma stopped stirring a pot of red chili sauce long enough to give her future daughter in-law a hug and a peck on her cheek.

Viv hoped Billy would be there before she left for her haircut, but he wasn't sitting in his normal booth. She frowned, but as she passed the booth, she spotted her fiancé's boots. He had lain down on the worn red vinyl seat and was snoring gently.

"Dahling let the poor man alone."

"I wasn't going to bother him Greta. Look at him, he's exhausted."

"He is kid, now go."

"Fine fine." She whispered.

Dad was sweeping the welcome mat

outside. "Off to the spa, boss lady?" He grinned.

"Not yet, need a haircut dad." She flipped her hair.

"Damn hippies! Tell'em I said hi."

"Will do."

She pulled into the tiny barbershop parking lot, but before she could open her door, a beat up old pickup shot into the space next to her. It came in too fast, and the right front wheel jumped up on the ancient railroad tie that was used as a curb. Viv sat and giggled into her hands as she listened to Marv cuss himself out for being old and blind. He left the truck parked that way, opened his door and started the long process of walking the twenty feet into the barbershop.

"Let me help you Marv." Viv said as she stood next to his opened truck door.

"Ain't you sweet." He smiled. "This might take a while."

"I have time, no hurry." He leaned hard on her shoulder. He was a tall man, and her shoulder was the perfect height for a human crutch.

"You sure do smell good." Marv said.

"Thanks Marv."

"Let it go kid, even old men gotta flirt."

"I know I know."

Even with her help, it took five minutes to get him inside to a chair.

"That's cheating Marv." Johnny the barber yelled at his old customer.

"Watch it or I'll tan yer hide." Marv shot

back.

"Hi Vivika!" A chorus from her fan club sang out. Five elderly men, smiling like they had all just won free pinup posters of Rita Hayworth.

"Hi everyone." Somehow "her boys" were always in attendance when Viv came in for her monthly haircut. Five haircuts in six months, word gets around. Some went so far as to ask Johnny when she was scheduled for her next one. He laughed them off and told them he had no idea when Vivika would be in again. But they still managed to be there to greet her.

Viv found a two month old fishing magazine, the same one where she'd read an article on how to finesse Crappie out of deep water in the wintertime using small minnows. Whatever. The next article in the magazine was the test results of three different brands of bass boats. Yea.

She was next, after the five ahead of her. No one cared. Viv sat, read, and listened with her third ear to the conversations flying back and forth. They were more of the same: did ya hear about, yep, bad prostate, his grandkid got busted again, what about that damn sniper? The air fell silent. Viv sensed that was a taboo subject even for these hardened men, most of which were veterans of a least one war.

"Okay Vivika, you're up." Johnny pointed at her with a pair of scissors.

"Actually, Marv was the first one through the door." Viv replied.

Truth or Consequences

"No, sweetie, you go ahead. I can wait." Marv said.

"Are you sure?"

"Yup little missy, you go right ahead. Old Marv will just sit and wait for the next open chair." He seemed to settle deeper into the waiting room chair than possible.

Viv bounded across the floor and into the aged brown leather barber chair.

"You're looking a hundred times better than that first time you sat in this chair. Look how healthy your hair is. You're doing a good job, Vivika." Johnny laid on the compliments.

"I'm happy now. I feel safe, I'm eating well. I've put on ten pounds."

"Only ten." He teased her.

"About ten."

"I heard about the sniper on the police scanner last night. Did they call Billy in?"

"Yes. Poor guy didn't get home til just a little while ago. Totally exhausted." Viv dished.

"He find anything?" He half whispered.

"I can't say." Viv said.

"Oh top secret stuff huh?"

"No, he fell asleep in one of the booths at the restaurant before I could talk to him."

There were four sets of ears in the barbershop, not counting Viv's. One set listened more intently than the others.

As they spoke, Johnny scoured each man's facial expression and eyes.

"Well, working so hard, he'll feel better

getting away to Taos for a couple of days." Johnny said.

"How'd you hear about that?" Viv struggled not to blush.

"Robert was in a couple of days ago. Got a trim. I cleaned up his bushy eyebrows and that Pancho Villa mustache of his. I asked about you kids." He stopped snipping her hair and stepped in front of her, "And I better get an invitation to the wedding, young lady."

"You will, and so will Marv." She raised her voice.

"What?" Marv asked and turned in her direction.

"I said you'll get an invitation to our wedding." Still loud.

"You and Johnny getting hitched?" Marv looked confused.

"No silly, me and Billy." Viv and Johnny laughed.

"Billy, ya say? Good boy that Billy." Marv turned back to staring at the wall across the floor from where he sat.

Johnny spent another ten minutes snipping and shaping her hair. "All done Miss Stryker." He said, and with a flourish removed her hair cutting drape with a bow.

"Still eight dollars?" She asked.

"Yes ma'am."

"Here's for mine and use the rest for Marv's haircut, my treat Marv." Her voice going up on his name.

"What's that?"

"My treat for your haircut today Marv." She practically shouted to him.

"Fine fine."

"See you next time Vivika." Johnny said brushing off the back of the chair and seat of the barber chair. "You're up Marv." Johnny called out.

Marv heard that with no problem, stood and started his walk to the chair. Viv stopped in front of him and gave him a hug.

"There there young lady. Let's not do this in public." He chuckled at his old man joke.

"You stinker." Viv playfully slugged him in the arm. His arm was as hard as a telephone pole. One tough old veteran.

She got into her car and looked in the rearview mirror and her haircut. It was great. She felt a little dizzy.

"Viv has a new boogeyman. Skip, skip, skip."

"What did you say Rebecca?"

"Kid, you need to tell Billy."

"About who? Who is the new boogeyman?" The dizziness was coming on stronger and her stomach flip flopped.

"Viv and the boogeyman, k, i, s, s, i, n, g."

Viv opened the car door, bent over and vomited.

"Kid, you really need to tell Billy."

The dizziness passed quickly, and she was

able to drive away. Viv wanted something cold to drink. She wanted a damn Slurpee, and since she hadn't had one in three weeks, it was time. She headed straight for her Slurpee connection at the convenience store, got a 32oz cup and mixed Banana and Blueberry together, then went out and sat at the picnic table in the cool shade. After 10oz, she was close to feeling normal. One more trip inside the store for a bag of Corn Nuts, and she washed them down with the rest of the Slurpee. And she was back to 100%.

Chapter 31

Over the next five days, Rebecca, Greta and Grumpy's voices turned into the drone of a broken record.

"Dahling, isn't it malvelous."

"You need to tell Billy."

"Booooooogeyman, Viv's got a new boogeyman. Skip, skip, skip."

Every time Viv heard Boogeyman, a spate of dizziness would follow. Fleeting but annoying. She had had enough.

"Billy, we need to talk." Viv spoke into her cell phone.

"Babe, what's the matter?" Billy, with his growing knowledge of Viv's nuances, knew something major was wrong.

"When you get off work today, can we drive up to Ranger's Lookout, the star gazing place?"

"Anything you want. Can you tell me what's going on?"

"When we get up there, I'll tell you everything."

"Okay babe." He glanced at the digital clock on the dash. "I should be at the restaurant in about an hour."

"Perfect. Billy..."

"Yes?"

"I love you."

"I love you too. You've got me worried

now."

"It should be fine, but I'm a little scared."

From 3:30 pm to 5 pm, the retirees from around the area would find their way to the restaurant for an early dinner, more to miss the crowds than any discounts or early to bed plans. Marv and Johnny drove into the parking lot at the same time. Viv was still in the front of the house, sitting alone in Billy's favorite booth.

"Boogey boogey, mannnnn. Skip, skip, skip."

Viv was instantly awash in a cold sweat, and something bubbled up her throat. She dashed to the restroom before she could greet her two favorite senior citizens.

"Marv, when are you going to get a new truck?" Johnny harassed his friend of too many years to count.

"Johnny? Is that you?"

"I got hungry, and Barb had to pull a double shift at the hotel. Let me give you a hand old timer."

"I'll old timer yer ass." Marv cracked a smile.

By the time Viv pulled herself together, the two elder customers were seated and ordered their meals.

"Viv, are you alright?" Johnny asked her, deep concern in his tone.

"Oh I'll be fine. Must have been something I ate."

"Booooooooogey MAN. Skip, skip,

skip."

"I hope not here!" Marv said and slapped the table top laughing.

"Excuse me fellas." She bolted for the bathroom again.

"Poor thing." Johnny said as he slipped another tortilla chip in a vessel of Momma's salsa. She had given him the recipe, and it was simple and quick: 1 large can of whole tomatoes, one or two fresh de-veined and seeded jalapeno peppers, half of a white onion, half a cup of parsley or cilantro, couple dashes of cumin, dash of crushed red peppers, couple good dashes of Cheyenne and chili powder, good pinch of salt and garlic salt, hit the chop button on the blender, let it whirl around until onions are tiny pieces, all done. But he could never make it taste like hers. Johnny assumed there was a secret spice missing, but he didn't take into account her thirty years of making it almost daily. Practice makes perfect.

"Okay Rebecca, I'm sick to death of this boogeyman crap. Are you trying to tell me that Johnny or Marv is a boogeyman?" She sat on the toilet with the waste basket between her knees. Silence from the voices.

"How about you Grumpy? Can you shed some light on this boogeyman thing?"

"Sorry kid, it ain't my area of expertise."

"How about you Greta?"

"Dahling it's wonderful news."

"About the boogeyman?"

Silence again. "If you guys aren't going to

help, then just shut the hell up!"

"Viv, are you ok?" Momma heard Viv talking loud in the bathroom.

"Fine, fine Momma."

"Let me see you." Momma twisted the doorknob, and opened the door to the one seater women's bathroom. Viv looked up at her with flushed cheeks and puffy eyes. She took one look at the waste basket. "Awwwwww. Come here you poor child. I'm so happy for you and Billy."

Momma snatched her up off the toilet. The waste basket fell away. "Happy for us why?" Light headed but standing, she accepted Momma's teary hug with confusion.

"Your pregnancy silly!"

"I'm not pregnant, Momma!"

"Have you told Billy yet?" Momma crushed her tighter to her bosom.

"Told Billy what? That I puke several times a day..." It finally hit her. She was pregnant.

"Dahling I told you it was great news!"

"Way to go kid! I hope he turns out taller than you did!"

"Robert! Robert!" Momma shouted as she pulled Viv from the ladies room.

Dad could tell from Momma's voice that whatever was going on, it was urgent. He stopped wiping down an oversized broiler pan, and it fell off the kitchen counter as he scrambled from the kitchen. "What's wrong?" He shouted. He met Momma and Viv as they came out of the hallway

Truth or Consequences

leading to the bathroom. "Our Viv is pregnant!!!" Momma said it loud and proud. The smattering of early evening customers heard the announcement and started clapping and cheering for them.

"Oh my god! Viv, is this true?" Dad put his arm around her and guided her to the nearest chair.

"I think it is. I haven't taken a test or anything." Pregnant? Me? Now?

"Does Billy know yet?" Dad repeated Momma's question.

"No. I just found out my damn self." The three of them hugged, laughed and cried, then hugged some more. Dad turned away and wiped tears from his eyes. Momma wouldn't let go of her hug on Viv. Viv didn't mind. She felt like the only thing keeping her from falling off the world was Momma's warm embrace.

Marv and Johnny cheered Viv on, lifting their glasses of iced tea toasting the happy news.

"I remember when Barb told me she was pregnant. Best and scariest damn news I ever had." Johnny said to Marv. "I don't think I've heard you mention any children Marv."

"Eh, well, I had a kid once." He looked misty eyed. Johnny knew better than to pursue the details.

"Well, here's to the dads of the world!" Johnny clinked glasses with his old dinner buddy.

Marv exchanged clinks with Johnny. "Excuse me for a few minutes Johnny boy."

Marv rose from his chair on rickety legs.

"You ok Marv?" Johnny asked.

"I just need to go out for some air, alone." Marv gave Johnny a stay-put-look.

"Oh, ok Marv."

Marv staccato stepped his way from the ebullient crowd. He eventually made it to the front door and outside. He went to the back of his truck. He lingered, fighting a tear, and jabbed his cane hard into the parking lot surface.

The happy and rowdy crowd inside cheered as Robert brought two unopened bottles of tequila from the kitchen and Momma brought a tray of shot glasses out for everyone. Marv stood his ground. Bunch of damn noise.

Billy pulled his truck into an open parking space, several down from where Marv was standing hunched at the shoulders, looking down at the ground.

"Hey Marv, you ok?" Billy asked as he approached.

"Sure, sure, just fine. You better get in there. They're acting like fools."

Billy heard a burst of voices, happy and loud. "What the heck's going on in there, Marv?"

"You'll have to find out fer yourself. Damn bunch of drunk fools if'n ya ask me."

Confused, and curious, Billy ventured inside. Viv was seated on a chair in the center of the restaurant, customers surrounding her. Dad was pouring shots as he walked around the circle. Momma stood near Viv, crying.

"What's gong on here?" Billy's voice quieted the revelers.

"Shhh, Billy's here." One customer instructed.

Viv motioned for Momma to come close. "I think we should be alone when I tell Billy, don't you?"

"Yes, yes. Ok everybody, break it up, the party is over. Viv needs to see Billy by herself."

"Viv?" Billy shrugged his shoulders.

"Are you ready to go up to the star gazing spot?"

"Sure, but isn't someone going to tell me what's going on here?"

"When we get up there, ok babe?" He noticed Viv was pale.

"Fine, let's go then." Billy said.

Viv went to her room. She wanted the perfect thing to wear when she told Billy the news, plus she decided it was time to tell him, in detail, about Rebecca, Greta, and Grumpy.

Marv regrouped and made it back to the table where Johnny was seated.

"I've had enough of this bull butter. I'm going home." Marv said.

"Can you give me a ride home Marv? I had nine or sixteen shots of takillya."

"Hell, I guess so." Marv laid a crisp fifty dollar bill on the table to cover both dinners and an out of character sloppy tip of thirty dollars. Johnny noticed that Marv wasn't waiting for his change. Even with a senior discount, Marv complained about his five damn dollar haircuts.

Marv pulled out of the parking lot, his drunken barber sitting next to him. Marv laid a heavy boot to the accelerator peddle. He sprayed gravel and created a huge dust cloud.

"Whoa, what's the hurry Marv?" Johnny asked.

"My foot slipped. You just sit back, I have an errand to run." Marv glared at Johnny.

"You feeling all right there Marv?"

"Just be still."

"Fine."

* * * * *

Billy was losing his patience. Viv was taking forever back in her room. What he didn't know was that Momma was counseling her on the right way to tell Billy about her "condition." They sat side by side on the bed, and Momma patted Viv's knee while they talked.

Dad walked up to Billy and offered him a full shot glass.

"No thanks dad. What's taking them so long?"

"Girl talk. They'll be out here in a few minutes."

Another twenty minutes passed before Billy and Viv were on their way to the star gazing point.

Chapter 32

"What the hell are we going up here?" Johnny's words came out wrong. "I mean what the hell?" The takillya swept him away.

"Don't worry about it. I told you I have an errand to run. Just sit back and relax."

Johnny hadn't been up to the ranger lookout since, hell, he couldn't remember the last time.

Marv guided the truck past the gate and snickered when he drove next to the "Authorized Vehicles Only" sign. He let his truck creep up the washed out battered access road. Marv had been at the ranger's lookout as recently as the day before, trying out the road and assessing the layout of the flat rocky area. He crossed the lookout and drove to the far edge to park.

"Now Marv, don't get no romantic ideas." Johnny cracked himself up.

Marv ignored his passenger, got out of the truck, stretched, and walked without the aid of his cane to the passenger door where Johnny sat looking out the windshield at the view of the lake. Marv opened the truck door. Johnny looked at him. Marv reached in with his right hand, grabbed Johnny by the shirt collar and, with one movement, jerked him out of the cab of the truck and threw him to the ground in a heap.

"What the hell are you doing Marv?" Johnny bypassed the fact that Marv yanked him out of the truck with little effort.

"Shut up." Marv reached into the truck again, flopped the back of the bench seat forward and pulled out a rifle case and a plastic garbage bag of mesquite branches.

Johnny struggled and tried to stand up. Marv removed the rifle from the case and struck Johnny in the back of the head with the butt of the gun. "I said shut up asshole." He bent down and took Johnny by his belt. He half dragged and half carried his limp body over to a boulder and propped him up against the side of it. He opened the bag of mesquite and poked a sprig into Johnny's left boot, put another into the rifle case, and slipped another tiny shred of the bush into the tripod that was installed at the bottom of the rifle stock.

Marv jogged back to the truck, closed the door, and backed up, then pulled forward up the fire access road that serpentined its way toward the top of the hill on the far side of the ranger's lookout. He stopped when the truck was out of the line of sight of anyone coming up the access road. Before leaving his truck, he reached under his front seat and pulled out a .44 magnum pistol. Marv jogged back down the hill away from his truck and back to Johnny's side, squatted down, and waited for Billy and Vivika.

* * * * *

Billy and Viv drove in silence from the

restaurant to their star gazing outpost. He noticed a super fine cloud of dust ahead of him as he drove the beat-up access road to the point above. It struck him odd, but he paid little attention to the possibilities of the cause. His attention was on Viv. To say he was nervous was an understatement. He maneuvered his powerful truck around the point, and came to a rest with the truck facing toward Elephant Butte Lake.

"Ok, let's talk." Billy said.

"I want the blanket so we can sit under the open sky."

"Fine." Barely hiding his exasperation.

She got out of the truck, and he pulled the blanket out from behind the front seat, found a spot, shook it open, and let it flutter to the ground. He looked at her, palms up, for approval.

"That's better. Come, sit." Viv sat down and patted the blanket next to her.

After Billy sat down next to his soon to be bride, Marv started his silent and deadly movement toward the couple. The night air was clean, crisp, and calm. Marv was within ear shot in seconds, and overheard every word Viv spoke to Billy.

"Eeny meany miny moe, the boogeyman is here. Skip, skip, skip."

Viv turned her head away from Billy, "Not now Rebecca."

"Pay attention kid!"

"Not you too Grumpy?"

"Who in the world are you talking to,

babe?" Billy asked.

"That's just one of the things I wanted to talk to you about. I have three voices that talk to me all the time." She took a deep breath, the confession lifted a weight from her.

"Ok, so I'm going to marry a crazy girl." Billy giggled. Not funny was the look on her face.

"These voices have names, Rebecca is a little girl skipping rope. Greta is like Greta Garbo in a silver lame' gown, leaning back on some sort of sofa. And then there is Grumpy. He's like a poster child for grandpas, overalls, and a torn up John Deere tractor hat covered in sweat stains. I don't see them like some of the ghost story shows on TV. Their voices come to me, kind of like having headphones on."

"I'm listening."

"They are spirits. They tell me things, not in super detail, but things, and I talk back to them."

"You're telling me that when I sat down here Rebecca and this Grumpy were talking to you?"

"Yes."

"What did they say?"

"Rebecca has been on this kick lately of telling me that I have a new boogeyman."

"A boogeyman?" He had heard some wild stories from speeders and drunk drivers, but this was by far the best.

"Yes. When Stromberg showed up, she

Truth or Consequences

was non-stop with this boogeyman stuff. Today at the barber shop, she started up again. I helped Marv out of his truck, and walked him to the door."

"She's telling you Marv is the new boogeyman?"

"Yes, and Grumpy said I needed to pay close attention. I get the sense that Marv has something to do with the sniper."

"That old man? No way!" Billy's voice dripped with distain for the theory.

"Booooooogey man."

"She just said it again. She sounded scared."

"What's that mean?"

"Usually I get the feeling she means that he's close by."

Billy rose up a little, craned his neck, and looked in all directions. "We're pretty much alone." The dust cloud crossed his mind, but he dismissed it quickly.

"Have you investigated Marv?"

"He's never showed up on the radar as far as a suspect. You've seen him walk. Good lord Viv, he's in his nineties!" "It has to be Marv. You're going to want to check him out."

"Good job kid."

"Grumpy agrees." Viv added.

"He just spoke to you?" Billy asked.

"Yes."

"Dahling will you pleeeeeeese get to the point."

244

"And what I really wanted to tell tonight was," She bit her lip.

"Well?"

"I'm pregnant." She didn't know what to expect from him.

"You're what? Wait. What did you just say? Pregnant?" He stammered and stuttered. "You're pregnant? How? When?" He jumped to his feet. "We'll have to get a place of our own. We have to get married tomorrow. Oh my god Viv, you're pregnant!!!" He reached down and pulled her to her feet. "Oh oh oh, I'm sorry are you ok?" He gently tried to sit her back down on the blanket.

"I'm fine. I take it this is good news? You're ok with being a father before you're a husband?"

"Oh my god you beautiful beautiful silly woman. I love you and I couldn't be happier!" He let go a loud war cry into the changing night sky. "Oh my god." He sank to one knee and hugged her tight and cried.

"BOOGEYMAN!!!" Rebecca screamed at Viv.

Viv shoved Billy off of her and stood up again. "He's here, he's right here!" Billy rolled over on the blanket, tears in his eyes.

"Who?" Shocked by her antics.

"Marv."

"Damn Billy, she's a better detective than you are!" Marv stepped from behind the truck.

Billy's eyes went right to the cannon of a

weapon in Marv's hand. "What's going on Marv?"

"I'm finishing up my work."

"What work is that Marv?" Billy asked.

"Tying up loose ends."

"He's going to kill us Billy." Viv said.

"Johnny too kid."

"And he's planning on killing Johnny. He's here somewhere. Marv is going to make it look like Johnny was the sniper."

"Damn you're good." Marv complimented her.

"He's going to shoot us with the rifle, and then he's going to use your gun, Billy, to kill Johnny. Nice and neat. Cop finds sniper, they fight, and everybody dies. Is that about right, Marv?" Viv said.

"That's the plan."

Billy looked at Viv, stunned. "Did your spirits tell you all of this?"

"Yes."

"I don't know about all of that, but she's a damn sight smarter than I gave her credit for." Marv said.

"Hey kid, Johnny's not dead yet. He's coming to help. Move off the blanket." Grumpy helped as he could.

Viv started a slow move, edging off of the blanket. She slowly ushered Billy off of the blanket to their right, creating an angle of attack for Johnny, from under Marv's line of sight. As she moved, she could make out a dark form about eighty feet to the rear of the truck. Johnny was coming out of the rifle conk on the head.

Johnny rubbed his forehead, then his temples. He touched the back of his head and came away with a bloody palm. He blinked several times, trying to regain some focus. Lots of blurring. His depth perception was all wrong as he looked around he made out Marv's tall frame, and two smaller frames in front of him. He was arguing, no, more like scolding the other two people. With his rattled senses, he thought he heard Viv's voice. Billy and Viv were up here?

"Kid, Johnny is going to make his move, be ready."

"Let me get this straight. You're the one that has been shooting? And you killed those people? You, a 92 year old half crippled son of a bitch?" Billy was copping an attitude.

Marv jumped off the ground and clicked his heels and danced a quick jig. "Yes, Officer Montez, one in the same."

Billy and Viv were blown away with his antics. From his vantage point, Johnny couldn't put Marv's voice to the jumping jackass in front of him. "Can't be Marv, but it's his voice."

"Something doesn't make sense here dammit." Billy upped his tone a notch.

"Here Officer Montez, check it out for yourself." Marv took out his wallet and tossed it to Billy.

Billy caught the wallet and unfolded it. In the fading daylight, Viv and Billy looked at

Marv's driver's license. They read the date of birth, and looked at Marv. He grinned. They re-read the date of birth, 11-24-46! They looked at Marv in total disbelief.

"But, but you, you act so old." Billy said.

"Exactly Officer Montez, I act old!"

"But, how, why?" Viv asked.

"A few skin grafts after I was jacked up in Viet Nam, and this damn desert sun turns people into prunes. About ten years back, I twisted my ankle out here hiking. Took me a while to get down off the mountain, two days in the sun to be exact. I finally made it to the emergency room and I looked like hell. My ankle hurt for damn near six months. I went into a store one day, and someone thought I needed help getting a shopping cart and moving around in the store. Treated me with respect, treated me like I was an old man. I overheard a couple of people guessing that I was in my eighties. I'm a victim of premature aging, and use it to my advantage." He smiled and spun around. "I'm fine."

"Hey kid, don't worry he won't shoot you with that cannon, it'll screw up his plan."

Viv advanced toward Marv.

"Back up little girl." Marv commanded pointing the pistol more directly at her.

"Marv, I've never done any thing to you, or disrespected you in anyway. You're not going to shoot me."

"Back the hell up now!"

In the background, Johnny made it to his

hands and knees, head throbbing so bad he thought his eyes would pop out of their sockets. His hand found a fat grapefruit sized rock.

Viv crept forward.

"Billy, tell your girlfriend I'll shoot. You've seen what I do to bodies."

"Viv, get back here." Billy said stepping to her side to pull her back. She refused to turn back or stop moving.

"Marv, why did you kill those people?" Viv finally found a stopping place and stared into his eyes, waiting for an answer.

"They helped kill my son, that's why!"

"What? How? You had a son?" Billy demanded an answer.

"My son got arrested for DUI," his voice wavered, and he lowered the gun slightly as he spoke, "The cops found an Elk in the bed of his truck. He poached it, and he had a little pot in his pocket. It went to trial. Those four bastards I killed were on the jury that convicted him. He was sentenced to two years for that bullshit. Little Mike was never a big kid. Not a runt mind you." A pang of fatherly pride. "But a few convicts got together and raped my boy. He was nineteen damn years old. He couldn't handle it and hung himself in his cell."

"And you blame the jury?" Viv asked.

"Hell yes. They had a choice of lesser charges, but they wanted the max!"

"They had no control over your son's stay in prison. That would have been up to the judge."

Billy said.

"Don't worry, he's still on my list."

Johnny dragged himself to within ten feet of Marv's back. He heard every word of Marv's speech. He raised the rock up high. Billy's eye flicked to the side. Marv saw the eye movement and turned to see Johnny with the rock crashing down, firing the pistol wildly as the rock made contact with the side of his skull.

Chapter 33

Johnny spent six days in the Intensive Care Unit. His personal physician explained to Barb, that the concussion was bad enough, that it alone could have taken his life. But with the gunshot wound from the .44 caliber hand-cannon, they had little confidence in Johnny's recovery. She should be prepared for brain damage at a minimum and many months of physical rehab for the gunshot wound to his shoulder. They had to monitor him closely for any signs of a stroke and infection.

Viv made daily trips to the hospital in Las Cruces to visit Johnny. Billy made the trip with her when his shift would allow. Barb took a leave of absence from the hotel with the owner's blessing. Viv made sure Barb had enough income in the interim.

Marv made a full recovery. He was facing more lethal charges than his son: four counts of capital murder, seven counts of attempted murder, and kidnapping. The D.A. expected a speedy trial.

* * * * *

Viv was "due" any day when she re-opened Bill and Edith's hot springs under its new name. As an ode to the huge waterfall she had constructed in the center of the circle drive, she re-named the business Stryker Falls Mineral Hot Springs and Spa.

Portia held her grand opening on the same day. Her first patient was Johnny the barber. His recovery was spectacular. He had suffered no brain damage, and with Portia's expert hands and techniques, along with the hot springs, his shoulder returned to full function in no time.

Billy and Viv had a simple marriage ceremony on the shore of Elephant Butte Lake, with a reception at Momma and Dad's restaurant.

More than half the town showed up for Viv's grand re-opening celebration. Claudia was one of the first through the door, critiquing the remodel. She sniped to her companion with each step she took.

Viv greeted as many people as she could as they arrived for the open house. Billy had to work later than he wanted to, but he showed up for the toast that the mayor insisted on giving to the new business.

Viv took Billy aside from the hubbub, and ended up in the kitchen off the office, just past the ten bistro tables covered in white linen. She was pulling him hard by the hand, "What's the big deal, Viv?"

"Two things. First," she stopped just a step outside the kitchen. "check this out." They stood before a dark purple satin draped object.

"What's this?" Billy asked.

"You'll see, close your eyes."

He did as he was told.

She tugged the satin drape off.

"Ok, open your eyes!"

"You're kidding me right?" Billy couldn't believe his eyes, but his new wife constantly surprised him. He was standing in front a brand spanking new Slurpee machine, cups and all. Blueberry and Raspberry flavors. On the right hand side of the machine, on a countertop, a wire rack of assorted flavors of Corn Nuts.

"You like?" Viv asked, grinning ear to ear.

"Hell yes. You are something else. Come here." He took her in his arms, "I love you Vivika Montez!" They kissed.

"Dahling get ready."

"I'm getting a baby brother. Skip, skip, skip."

"What was the second thing babe?" Billy asked reminding her.

"I think I finally know who I am."

"Way to go kid."

Made in the USA
Charleston, SC
01 October 2010